Come Away with Me
The Andrades

Ruth Cardello

Come Away With Me
The Andrades

By Ruth Cardello
Copyright © 2014 Ruth Cardello

First Printing, 2014, Paperback edition 1.0
ISBN: 978-1497426993

Print cover by Gilded Heart Designs

Author Contact
Website: RuthCardello.com
Email: Minouri@aol.com
Facebook: Author Ruth Cardello
Twitter: RuthieCardello

Dedication:

I am so grateful to everyone who was part of the process of creating *Come Away with Me*. Thank you to:

Christy Carlyle at The Gilded Heart Design for my new cover.

My very patient beta readers: Luci Hurd, Yeu Khun, Karen Lawson, Renita Lofton McKinney and Cynthia Pak.

My editors: Karen Lawson, Janet Hitchcock, Nina Pearlman, and Margaret Rainforth.

My three year old daughter who feels that she's helping when she sits on my lap while I review edits. Although she doesn't understand a comma's function, she's sure I need more of them.

Melanie Hanna, for helping me organize the business side of publishing.

My Roadies for making me smile each day when I log on my computer.

Thank you to my husband, Tony, who listens to the story so many times he dreams about the characters.

To my niece, Danielle Stewart, for joining me in self-publishing and brainstorming with me along the way. *Always better together.*

A note to my readers:

The Andrade family has had a special place in my heart since they first appeared in *For Love or Legacy*. I'm the youngest of eleven children. Although we didn't have money, I based the Andrades on what it was like for me to grow up with so many relatives.

My parents are no longer with us, but they were happily married for almost sixty years. My mother was the storyteller in our family. She was notoriously funny. My father was much more reserved, but he loved her sense of humor. Even when they were in their eighties, if my mother told a joke, my father would look on with a smile.

Our dining room table was a long L-shaped counter that was actually purchased from a local diner that had gone out of business. With so many children, one would think that my parents wouldn't allow us to bring friends home with us for meals, but they believed the exact opposite—friends were family to us. I often had meals with twenty or more people. For those who have read the Legacy Collection, that's where I got my philosophy that love is a fountain—where there is always enough for those who have stayed and those who return to it.

My parents taught me that family and friends are what matters the most, children should always be valued, and forgiveness is the greatest kindness you can give one another. I miss them every day, but I like to think that they live on through how I am raising my own children.

No family is perfect.

Gio, Nick, Luke and Max are on a difficult journey that will test what they think they know about loyalty and love. I hope you enjoy this series. I've fallen in love with these lost Andrades and the story of how they find their way back to their family.

Chapter One

IF YOU WANT a dose of reality, come home a day early.

Gio Andrade walked through his secretary's empty office and into his, shaking his head with disgust as he went. He double-checked the time on his watch. Barely seven o'clock. She should still be here. Someone should be here. Rather than call her, he sank into the antique leather chair placed behind the custom Carpathian elm desk that had sat in this office for generations.

Perhaps it was the combination of three weeks of travel and spending so much time in hotel rooms, but he was tired. Bone tired and in a foul mood. He'd gone on site in northern Canada to make sure the project met its deadlines, and it did—something that normally would have energized him. Instead, he felt distracted.

He didn't consider himself an emotional man. Ever since he'd taken over the family's company, his success had come from his ability to remain detached. Cogent Energy Solutions had been born in the oil wells of Texas, but Gio had taken it in a much different direction. He was an investor, not a developer. He found potential energy sources—like the Utica Shale veins recently discovered in North America—that others considered economically unfeasible to reap, financed the breakthrough technologies that would make harvesting them possible, contracted with companies who needed those sources, made a huge fortune, and then got out before the environmentalists even knew his name.

Clean.

Calculated.

Satisfying.

Until this past trip.

What is wrong with me?

His cell phone vibrated in his breast pocket. He checked the caller ID and groaned. It was his cousin Madison Andrade. Again. Her calls were becoming more frequent. He'd answered the first couple. Forwarded the next few to his secretary, Rena. Now he let her calls ring through to voice mail. Part of him was beginning to admire her tenacity, even as he remained unwilling to consider her request.

He placed the phone down on his desk and started sifting through the large pile of mail that had accumulated in his absence. Rena had opened and dealt with most of it, but one square ivory envelope was still sealed. He picked it up and turned it in his hand. He already knew what it was. Madison had told him to expect an invitation to Stephan Andrade's wedding.

An Andrade wedding.

What a joke. We may share the same last name, but that's all we have in common.

Gio crushed the invitation, still unopened, into a ball and threw it in the wastebasket beside his desk. *My mistake was reopening any communication with that side of the family. I have Luke to thank for that.*

Gio didn't speak to Luke often, but that lack of contact had more to do with their schedules than anything else. Of his three brothers, Luke was the easiest to get along with. He was a respected doctor and someone who never asked for anything, so Gio had been hard-pressed not to accept his request to join him at a high-profile function a few months earlier.

The event ended up being an engagement party for a couple he didn't know, much less care about. The unpleasant bonus had been the presence of two uncles he'd spent nearly a decade avoiding. He'd left as early as he could without seeming rude, and had made his excuses while interacting as little as possible with any of his extended family.

I should have told Luke I was out of the country that week.

I should have lied.

Gio's phone beeped to announce the message his cousin had left. *By going to that party, I mistakenly gave some family members the wrong idea.*

Now they think I care. I don't.

The days when what they do or say have any relevance to me are long gone. He would have said as much to Madison, but she had done nothing to him. As the frequency of her calls increased, however, he began to feel pushed into an uncomfortable situation. No one likes to shove a puppy away, but when it starts humping your leg, you have to.

Gio covered his eyes with one hand at the image. *Oh, my God. I am tired.*

Still too tense to consider heading home to bed, he loosened his tie and strode over to the office bathroom. His office was his home away from home, and the shower and assortment of clothing in its large closet was evidence of that.

He changed from his Kiton suit into his workout clothes and running sneakers. He'd had a full gym installed on the top floor of the Cogent Building, and he'd made it available to all his employees.

Not that anyone would be taking advantage of it that night, since the building was apparently empty. He took that irritation to the treadmill and started running, welcoming the initial discomfort as his tight muscles were pushed to stretch and perform. *Pain is weakness leaving the body. Best to work through it.*

As I always have.

An hour later, after completing a long run and doing a circuit of weights, Gio grabbed a towel and headed back down to his office. His blood was pumping and his mood had improved. Half-smiling, he considered calling one of his usual friends with benefits.

He reentered his secretary's office, then swore when he realized he had closed the door to his office, effectively locking his cell phone, keys, and everything else inside.

What the hell?

He picked up Rena's phone and called down to the security desk, but it rang repeatedly without being answered. Heads would roll the next morning.

Looking down at his secretary's desk, he noted the calendar. *September 1. Labor Day. No wonder the offices are empty.* It didn't explain the absent security, but it did reinstate his opinion of his usually dedicated secretary.

Angry for allowing himself to become distracted enough to lose track of the day, he impatiently searched the top of her desk. *Rena must have a key to my office.*

He tried the drawers of her desk but they were locked. Which made sense, he supposed. He wouldn't have appreciated if the key proved easily accessible. Still, her competence wasn't helpful at the moment.

Losing patience, he tugged at the top drawer more aggressively.

∞

Seated at a security console in a small room on the Cogent Building's first floor, Julia Bennett neglected watching the monitors in favor of checking her makeup in her compact mirror. She hoped her brown hair held a sophisticated amount of curl. She still had the top of her security uniform on, but there wasn't much she could do about that for—her eyes flew to the clock on the wall—thirty more minutes.

She let out a nervous breath and smoothed her hands down the tight black skirt that ended a few inches above her knees. She glanced down at her Marc Jacobs four-inch heels, shoes that would not pass dress code, but would have to for one night. In twenty minutes, she would replace her tan blouse with a much bolder red silk one.

Red was a power color.

And she needed all the mojo she could muster.

The door to her security cave opened and Paul, one of the front-desk security men, shuffled in. He was a couple of years older than Julia and, due to the number of hours he put in at the gym each day, nearly twice her size. "Julia, can you cover the front desk for me for a few minutes? I have to run across the street to the pharmacy. I won't be long."

Shit.

"Paul, I don't even know how to sign someone in."

"You won't have to. It's a holiday. No one is here. No one is coming. Listen, normally I would never ask you to do this, but you know that I'm on by myself tonight. Tom has a stomach bug." The six-foot-six giant of a man looked more like a sad little boy when he added, "I think he gave it to me. I probably have a fever. Feel my head. Do I?"

Dutifully, Julia stood, walked over, and touched his forehead, noting that he did feel overly warm. She glanced at the clock. Twelve past. *Shoot.* "You might. Tell me what you need. I can run over and get it."

He shook his head. "No. I have symptoms I don't want to discuss." He gave her a sheepish smile. "I've been in the bathroom half the night."

Although Julia had only worked at Cogent for a little more than a month, Paul and Tom felt like old friends. Working overnight shifts had given them many opportunities to bond over the coffee breaks Julia still needed to keep awake. Normally her job consisted of nothing more than watching a panel of monitors and reporting anything unusual to Paul or Tom. Not the most exciting job, but one that paid the bills.

Everyone had been so nice to her that she felt guilty about not instantly agreeing to Paul's request. "Okay, go. But hurry back. I put in to leave early. I feel awful, but I'm meeting that buyer tonight. This could be it—what I came to New York for."

"Is this the same guy you told me about the other day?"

"Yes. He works for Platinum and Onyx. It has stores all over the world. An order from him could change everything for me. Now, go. I'll watch the desk."

When she walked by him, Paul said, "That skirt is short for a business meeting."

She frowned over her shoulder at him. "I'm not going to sell to anyone if I keep dressing like a small-town bumpkin. Trust me, I've researched power outfits. This one says, 'I'm a strong and vital woman. Buy my jewelry.' "

Paul looked unconvinced. "If you're meeting a guy, that skirt says, 'I'm hot, buy *me*.' "

Julia stomped one of her high heels in frustration. "To win in business, you have to take advantage of all of your assets. If he gets a little distracted by my skirt... well, that's the way of the jungle."

Shaking his head, Paul said, "Call me if he turns out to be a creep. One of my buddies will meet you." Having met some of his beefed-up friends, Julia had no doubt they would. They were brawn looking for a brawl.

"I won't have to because I'm fierce. I have my whole presentation ready. He will be so wowed by the items I show him, he won't have drool left for my legs." She hovered behind Paul's seat at the front security desk cautiously. *What are the chances he sanitized any of it?*

With a grunt of disapproval, Paul headed toward the large glass-door exit.

Julia couldn't stop herself from calling out, "Hurry, Paul. I can't be late."

Julia paced behind the desk and watched the clock. Tick. Tock. Tick. Tock. *Crap, I should have brought my clothes out here. I could change in the ladies' room while waiting.*

She sprinted back to the surveillance room to gather her things. While scanning the area to make sure she wasn't forgetting anything, she noticed something on one of the monitors: a door to one of the administrative offices was open. All offices were supposed to be closed and secured after the cleaning staff left. Paul would hear about it in the morning if nothing were done. *Don't forget to tell Paul about it. Don't forget. Crap, I'm going to forget.*

Back at the front desk, Julia couldn't stop thinking about that open door. *I can get up and back before Paul returns.*

She rushed to the elevator bank and pushed the button to the highest office floor. She flew across the carpeted hallway to the open office and had her hand on the doorknob when she noticed a tall man in sweatpants trying to break into the desk in the outer office.

She said the first thing that came to her head: "Halt right there."

The man slowly straightened to an impressive height and turned. Julia gripped the door handle tighter. Eyes as dark as coal slowly raked over her, as if they had every right to. Gorgeous eyes. Thick, dark hair that was tussled just enough to set a woman's imagination afire. Who knew burglars could be hot? *Yes, officer, I did tackle him, but I had to. It had nothing to do with those perfectly muscled shoulders and that flat stomach. I admit, we rolled around on the floor once or twice together, but purely so I could restrain him.*

Julia shook her head to clear it. *Down, libido, down. This is not one of those dreams where someone like him kisses someone like me, and I wake up frustrated and reach for my vibrator. This is reality, and even though he's gorgeous, he could still be dangerous.*

One of his beautiful eyebrows arched at her prolonged appraisal of him, then his gaze settled appreciatively on the exposed length of her legs. "And you are?"

"Security." She referenced her uniform and name tag. "You don't belong in here."

"You're security?" he asked incredulously. "The singing or the stripping kind?"

Instantly angry, Julia put a hand on one hip and demanded, "Do I look like a stripper?"

His eyes slowly, ever so slowly, roamed over her high heels, short skirt, and riotous head of hair.

She stomped a foot at his lack of appropriate response. "This is a power outfit." She looked down and tugged at her uniform top. "Not this. But it's coming off." When his eyes widened, her ire rose. "Not for you. And that's not what I meant. I have a beautiful red shirt that goes with this skirt. A nice conservative shirt. And this skirt is a perfectly appropriate length for a business meeting, according to *Entrepreneur Today*." She took a deep calming breath. "Why am I justifying my outfit to a possible criminal? I don't know what you're doing here, but you need to leave."

"Or what? What would you do?" He stepped closer.

Good question. Julia looked behind her, then back at him. *See, this is why I should have taken the salesperson job at the mall. But I thought, Night security—that will give me more time to read and network during the day. Where are you, Paul, when I need you? That's it. Paul.* "I won't have to do anything, because my partner is already on his way up. In fact, the next time that elevator opens, it'll be him, and he is twice your size and has taken just enough steroids to have a little rage, if you know what I mean. I'll do what I can to hold him off, but if he catches you, that gorgeous face of yours will never look the same."

A predatory smile stretched his lips. He closed the short distance between them, effectively pinning her against the wall between his arm and the door. "I don't believe you," he said, his voice deep and husky. He studied her as if he were trying to solve a puzzle. "Are you going to tell me what you're really doing here?"

Her voice tight in her throat, she said, "I told you. I'm security."

He opened his mouth to say something, and Julia lost control. Attraction peaked and collided with panic. Her frantically searching hand closed on a lamp on the table beside them. With one swift move she cracked him in the temple with it. He stumbled back and raised a hand to the assaulted area. "What the hell... ?"

They both froze. His eyes lit with a fire that set her heart racing.

In the doorway, a male voice broke in. "Mr. Andrade. Are you okay? What happened?"

Julia put the lamp down quickly and swayed a bit beneath the realization of what she had just done. "Mr. Andrade. As in, George Andrade?"

Still looming angrily over her, he said, "Gio. No one calls me George." He addressed Paul curtly. "She works here?"

"Yes, sir. For over a month."

Glittering black eyes bored into Julia as she smiled awkwardly back at him. "I didn't recognize you."

"Evidently." He rubbed the red mark on his left temple.

Paul stepped forward with concern. "I'm so sorry, sir. This is my fault. I ran next door to get medicine—"

Gio held up one hand to silence Paul, and the gesture proved impressively effective. In this jungle, money trumps muscle, Julia thought sarcastically. "We'll talk about it tomorrow. Right now—"

Tomorrow. Tonight. Time. Crap. Julia glanced at the clock. *Seven thirty. Shit.* She turned apologetically to Paul. "Oh, my God, Paul. I am so sorry. I'll take the heat for this. I promise. This was all my fault. Write it up however you need to. I would, but I can't stay. I'm already late."

She made the mistake of meeting the eyes of the man who still looked dazed from his encounter with the lamp. She instinctively reached toward his temple in sympathy, then dropped her hand. "I'm sorry. I should have studied the photo book Paul gave me better. It's just that you were dressed like... and then you were all..." She frowned. "You could have just told me who you were and none of this would have happened, but we don't have time to go into that now. Don't be mad at Paul, okay? He has a stomach bug. But normally, he'd die to protect you. Who else can you say that about?" She glanced quickly at the clock again and said, "I totally understand if you need to fire me, but can you do it tomorrow?"

She turned and fled.

After her whirlwind departure, Gio looked across at Paul. "Just tell me you didn't issue her a gun."

Chapter Two

JULIA STEPPED OUT of the taxi and onto the busy sidewalk in midtown Manhattan. She hesitated for a moment, reread the address she held in her hand, then squared her shoulders, shifted her jewelry-laden messenger bag higher on her shoulder, and strode toward the entrance of what appeared to be a bar.

A bar? And if the crowd in the windows was any indication, a popular one at that. Julia stepped inside and tried to remain optimistic. *With a live band? New Yorkers play by their own rules. Who needs to discuss business in an office when you can do it and watch live entertainment at the same time? This doesn't have to change anything. So, there won't be room for me to use the mini display case I made. I'll just show him individual pieces.* The band began to play a fast song with a heavy bass line that virtually shook the photos hung on the wall. People stood shoulder to shoulder, and Julia squeezed between gyrating couples as she searched for a familiar face.

The scene was worlds away from the small ocean-town bars Julia was used to, but she didn't let her determination waver. *I'll go to an office, to a bar... hell, I'll meet someone in a back alley... I don't care. I will sell my jewelry in New York. This crowd, that band—they won't stop me.*

A roving hand caressed her derriere as she squeezed between a cluster of inebriated men. She spun on the offender and grabbed him by the collar of his neck, pulling him down so she could speak directly into his ear. "I grew up in a neighborhood of all boys. I will seriously fuck you up if you touch me again."

It wasn't true, but it didn't have to be. Not according to *The Power of Believing,* a book she had purchased to cheer herself up back in Rhode Island—a book that had changed her life.

Want to succeed? Believe that you can. Want to intimidate someone? Believe that you are someone they should fear.

The drunken man took a step back and raised both of his hands in a move that showed he was backing away. That small triumph bolstered Julia's confidence. *I can do this.*

As she turned away from Mr. Wandering Hands, she saw Bill Pritt waving her over to a corner booth. She slid into the booth next to him with relief.

Dressed in an off-the-rack suit and tie, Bill looked exactly as she remembered him from the day she'd met him: a slightly out-of-shape businessman in his early forties. They'd both been hailing taxis on Fifth Avenue and, when one came, he'd offered to share the ride with her. A quick look at his left hand revealed he was married, and that had given Julia the reassurance she needed to join him. While the taxi navigated the heavy traffic, he'd asked her what brought her to the Diamond District, and the story of why she'd come to New York had spilled out of her.

She hadn't expected him to be interested, but he had listened attentively and then surprised her by telling her he worked for a large jewelry chain and was always scouting for new designers. They'd exchanged phone numbers and Julia had smiled her way through her shift that day. Their meeting had been a sign. Unable to help herself, she'd called everyone back home to tell them about the opportunity. *Now all I have to do is close the deal.*

Smiling down at her, he leaned in closer than she was personally comfortable with, but likely necessary given the deafening level of the music. "I was getting ready to leave. I thought you'd changed your mind."

Forcing a bright smile onto her face and shaking off the disaster the night had already been, Julia said, "Absolutely not. I was thrilled to get your call."

"I'm glad," he said and waved the cocktail waitress over. "Two dirty martinis."

"I don't actually..." Julia almost said "drink," then thought better of it. *What am I going to ask for? A soda? Why not go all out and order a Shirley Temple? Remember, sophisticated. Strong. Of course I drink martinis.* "Thank you."

When they were alone again, Julia said, "I brought all kinds of samples with me. These are in copper and aluminum with fake gemstones," she said, pulling a few pieces out of her bag. "I have a couple made with more expensive materials, but I don't like to carry them around with me. Of course, if you put in an order, all of these will be made with the highest quality materials I can afford." *Why did I add that last part? It makes me sound like... like who I am. An amateur.* "I mean..."

He put his left hand down on her thigh and gave it a suggestive squeeze. "Let's not talk business yet."

Julia sat up, grabbed his hand, and dropped it on the table as if it were a napkin that had fallen to the seat. The ring he'd worn the day they'd met was missing, but an indent was still visible. Julia's mood downshifted in stages: Confusion. Disbelief. Then finally, a growing understanding that was accompanied by an overwhelming surge of disappointment and anger. "I thought you were interested in my pieces."

"I am," he said, his eyes glittering with an interest Julia didn't welcome. "All of them."

Skin crawling, Julia scooted back and stood, shaking her head in revulsion. "You're married."

He reached forward and grabbed her forearm. "My wife doesn't care what I do."

Julia shoved at his hand. "Don't touch me."

He didn't release her. "Come on. Sit back down. You can show me what you brought with you if it's so important to you."

Just then, the cocktail waitress arrived with their drinks. With her free hand, Julia picked up one of the martinis and poured it over Bill's head. He released her arm and cursed loudly.

Opportunities only come when you're strong enough to take them on. This is good. It'll toughen me up. Before walking away, Julia said, "I'm not sorry I came here tonight. You know why? Because you just made me very angry, and anger is a motivating emotion." According to her second favorite book, *Stress to Success*. With that, she spun and pushed her way through the crowd, hoping her bravado wouldn't fail before she found the door.

When she approached the area where Mr. Wandering Hands was still standing, he stepped back and tapped his friends to do the same so she could pass. Bag clutched tightly and head held high, she walked through the path they'd opened for her.

"I told you she's feisty," Mr. Wandering Hands said to his friends. "I'm in love."

She paused and glared at him. "You'd have a much better chance with women if you didn't grab at them as they walk past."

He blushed and ducked his head, and Julia guessed he was much younger than whatever his ID claimed.

Perfect way to round off the day.

Groped by a teenager. Propositioned by a married man.

And don't forget probably fired.

Julia exited the bar, hailed a cab, and tried to stem the tears that were welling within her. *I'll grow from this tomorrow. Right now I just feel like an ass.*

I'm such an idiot. That guy is probably not even a jewelry buyer. Why did I think I could do this? I'm not a businesswoman. I don't belong in New York City. What the hell am I doing?

She entered her building and walked up the three floors to her tiny studio apartment. Her phone rang.

"Jules. I know I shouldn't call you tonight, but I figured if you were still in your big business meeting you wouldn't answer."

"Hi, Dad," Julia said sadly as she opened the door to her apartment, then closed it heavily behind her. She hung her bag on the wall hook, stepped out of her shoes, and walked toward her bed that doubled as her couch. "How's Mom?"

"She's doing well. We're hopeful about the new doctor we're using."

"That's good. That's really good. Is she awake?"

"No, hon. She already went to bed for the night. The medicine makes her tired, but she isn't as anxious when she gets confused. I told her you were doing well, and that made her happy. So, tell me. Which piece sealed the deal?"

Julia sank onto the corner of her bed and slumped forward. "I didn't get it, Dad. He didn't want my jewelry."

"Then he's an idiot. Don't give him a second thought." Julia almost smiled, remembering that her father had said close to the same thing about every boy she'd pined for since grade school. They didn't make many men like her father—gentle giants who loved with every fiber in them. Julia had always loved it when her mother spoke of how they'd met. Elizabeth had been driving home to the Carolinas, down the East Coast, after graduating from college and had planned to drive through Rhode Island without stopping. Her car had overheated within state lines, and he had pulled over to offer help. Flirtation had led to coffee. The story was a little vague after that, but her mother had never made it home. She'd stayed and married her father, and together they'd built the family business, Bennett Wood Creations, which was part showroom and part factory. Her father was a gifted furniture designer and craftsman. Her mother had excelled at finding buyers and keeping the books. They'd made a good team—an artist and a business-minded woman.

Until Mom got sick.

Flopping back into the thick, flowered comforter on her bed, Julia confessed, "I may have also been fired from my job today."

Just as she expected, her father's support didn't waver. "From the security gig? That's not a career anyway. It's a filler job. You'll have another one before you know it."

I wish I could believe that. "I don't know, Dad. What if I don't have what it takes to make it here?"

Her father cleared his throat. "You can always come home, Jules. You know that."

"All it would take to get the books current is one good deal, Dad. I have to try."

"It's just a business, Jules. It's not what matters." The sadness in his voice tore at Julia's heart. Her father would do anything for her and for his wife, but he wasn't a businessman. He'd tried to downplay the seriousness of his situation, but Julia knew how close he was to losing everything.

Her mother would have known how to turn it around. She would have known exactly what to say to the bankers, who had begun pressuring her father to sell the land to local developers before they claimed it and auctioned it off themselves. The hardest part of Alzheimer's was, although her mother was there, still laughing and playing cards with her father, the sharp woman she'd been was gone.

Leaving Dad and me to fend for ourselves.

And we were cut from the same dreamer cloth.

No, I will no longer limit myself with narrow definitions of who I am. I'm a reasonably intelligent person. I can learn to be a businesswoman.

I must have some of my mother in me.

It was that decision that had started Julia reading motivational business books. *Surround yourself with those you want to emulate. Want to land an opportunity? Put yourself where opportunities are plentiful. Want to be a business shark? Swim with sharks.*

Less than four hours from her home and boasting one of the world's largest collections of jewelry businesses, New York had been a natural choice for Julia. Working nights allowed her to frequent the Diamond District and learn which pieces were selling and which weren't. It was a culture shock, but not all bad. New Yorkers were sharply dressed, blunt in their speech, and willing to fight to death for a taxi. She respected them even as she struggled to keep up with them.

"It does matter, Dad. It matters to me."

"It's not a weight that belongs on your shoulders. I have some options I'm considering."

Julia sat up and wiped her tears away. "Don't do anything until I come home, Dad. This is going to work out. You and Mom have been the best parents anyone could ever ask for. I would still be selling my jewelry out of your furniture store if Mom hadn't gotten sick. You always believed in me."

"That's what parents do, Jules."

"No. Not all parents, Dad. Good parents. And I know I don't have to do this for you. I want to do this. I will do this."

With a voice that was thick with emotion, her father said, "New York is about to discover an incredible artisan. I believe that. You'll find a buyer. You know why? Because you have your mother's heart. She was always a scrapper. If this is what you feel you need to do, then you get back out there, Jules, and you fight for it. Not for Mom and me. But for you."

Wiping away a fresh tear, Julia said, "I will, Dad. I'll make you proud."

"I'm already proud, Jules. Now go get some rest. Tomorrow is a whole new day. Love you."

"Love you more," Julia whispered and hung up. She fell back onto her bed and covered her eyes with one arm.

It won't be hard for tomorrow to be better than today.

Although, today could have been worse. I could have accidentally killed Gio Andrade with that lamp instead of just stunning him. An image of her boss, eyes flashing with fury while he touched the wound on his temple, brought a fresh flush of color to her cheeks. Her breath caught as she remembered how he had looked when he'd turned around from his secretary's desk—so arrogant, so in control.

Well, I knocked that right out of him.

She groaned at the memory.

And then actually wondered if he was attracted to me.

Because nothing is hotter than a good ol' smack to the side of the head.

I'm sure he's lying in his ridiculously plush bed thinking about me tonight.

Yeah, right.

Oh, my God. I'm going to be arrested when I go to work tomorrow.

❧

Gio restlessly turned over in his bed. Another sleepless night. This time, however, he wasn't thinking about any of his international projects. Nor was he cursing his family for distracting him from more important matters.

No, tonight he was plagued by the image of a woman he had no business thinking twice about. If there was one rule Gio had always adhered to, it was never mix business with pleasure.

Rolling onto his back, he tested the tender skin on his bruised temple and winced. He should have told Paul to fire her on the spot. That crazy brunette was obviously completely unsuited for security work. Beyond not recognizing the owner of the business she was supposedly guarding, she was dangerously unpredictable.

A fact that didn't stop his cock from stirring to life at the memory of how her legs had seemed to go on forever. He shook his head and groaned as the movement sent a knifelike pain through his head. Still, his erection grew as his traitorous mind conjured images of what she would have looked like in just those high heels.

I should have let Ceci come over.

One of his welcome-home messages had been from his last hookup. She'd thanked him for the thoughtful gift he'd sent while he was away. He'd have to ask his secretary what it had been. He hoped she'd followed his normal rule of something generous that didn't promise anything more. The women he dated expected to be pampered, but they knew the score.

Sex was just sex.

And good sex, while necessitating the occasional diamond bracelet, did not require emotional investment or the hypocrisy of vows. Marriage might have made sense back when a person's life expectancy was forty, or when social norms dictated it, but he saw no reason for it in modern society.

Maybe for the sake of children.

But the world was already overpopulated—it could do with a few less of those, too. As his body continued to betray him and throb beneath the sheets, he rolled over again and punched one of his pillows. He didn't want Ceci; he wanted his little brunette security woman.

What was it about her that made her unforgettable? Was it the way she'd reprimanded him even after she knew who he was, seemingly unimpressed by his title and wealth? He couldn't remember a time when he'd been so easily dismissed by a woman. She'd seemed more concerned with upsetting Paul than him.

And I'm the one she hit.

That's probably all this is—a concussion.

If concussions come with the side effect of a raging hard-on.

His little security guard was beautiful, but beauty was common in his world. She was lean with a killer ass, but those were common traits, too. What had been novel was the way his gut had clenched with excitement whenever their eyes met. He wasn't an impulsive man, but he'd found himself cornering her, afraid she was an illusion conjured up by his exhaustion—a dream he didn't want to wake from.

Desire that intense is dangerous.

Complicated.

A weakness that topples empires.

Something I thought I was immune to.

I'm being ridiculous.

This is the result of too much work and several weeks of pent-up sexual frustration.

I'll call her into my office tomorrow, and in the light of day my cock will see the truth.

She's just a woman.

Nothing different than any other I've known.

Not worth risking anything for.

Chapter Three

"RENA, SEND JULIA Bennett up as soon as she gets in." He hated that he'd started his day unable to concentrate on his email and instead requested information on a woman he'd spent far too much of the night thinking, then dreaming, about.

He wasn't happy with himself for succumbing to his curiosity and asking for background checks ASAP on all of the new hires, merely so he could find out more about her. No one needed to know that hers was the only folder he intended to open.

He'd half hoped to discover something big enough to negate the building anticipation he felt as he counted down the hours until her shift started. Unfortunately, what he'd read had left him more, not less, intrigued by her.

Although she had no experience with security, her flowered and scented résumé had somehow won over the head of human resources. Julia's only prior employment had been at her family's furniture business, where she claimed to have created a jewelry department and listed her skills as: Ask me.

For the third time that day, he opened the small handwritten card that had been paper-clipped to her résumé. She had warmly thanked the woman she'd interviewed with and written, "I know I'm not the most qualified person for the position, but I can guarantee you that no one wants it more than I do. I will come in early. I will work late. I don't mind holidays or double shifts. Looking forward to hearing from you. Julia. P.S. I hope you don't mind that I included a box of peppermint tea. During the interview you expressed that your sinuses were giving you trouble. I had my father overnight my favorite herbal blend. Our family swears by it."

Since most of his business was conducted in the field, Gio wasn't normally concerned with the level of security at his headquarters, but he could see the error in that now. He'd have that unpleasant conversation with his security team later.

For now he replaced the card in Julia's folder and shook his head.

This isn't me.

I don't sit around waiting for any woman.

Certainly not someone who works for me.

But I need to see her again.

I need to prove to myself that what I felt last night can't be repeated. He hadn't realized how emotionally closed off he'd become until he'd looked into the eyes of a woman who had made him uncomfortably aware of it. What Julia made him feel was just as unwelcome as the sensation of pins and needles that fills a limb after it's been temporarily cut off from blood.

And as impossible to dismiss.

He practically jumped out of his chair when he heard a light knock on his door. Not since his first teenage crush could he remember his heart beating so wildly in his chest at the idea of seeing someone again.

Rena opened the door. "I have the soil analysis you asked me for." She stepped inside, placing them on his desk. Instead of leaving as she normally did, she hovered. "Are you feeling okay, Gio? Is your head still bothering you? I have some aspirin in my purse if you need it."

"I'm fine," Gio ground out. Rubbing a hand over the small red mark on his temple, he added, "Thank you."

"You asked me to remind you to call Mr. Atwater today. I did earlier, but his secretary called a few minutes ago. She wanted you to know he's in his office late tonight. I wasn't sure if that meant you had forgotten. I told her I'd tell you."

Cursing under his breath, Gio stood. "He can wait. He needs my investment more than I need the opportunity."

"Yes, sir." She went halfway to the door and stopped. "Miss Elson called this morning. I told her you were in meetings all day."

"Good. I broke it off with her before I left. I hope you sent her nothing more than the usual."

"The three-carat 'thank you now go away' bracelet that Tiffany's buys in bulk just for you? Sent it with the usual note," Rena replied blandly, still remaining in the room. It was times like this when Gio regretted hiring his friend Kane's sister as his administrative assistant. She was good at her job, but she often felt personally invested in things that were none of her business.

Gio leaned back against his desk and folded his arms across his chest. "Say it."

"Aren't you getting tired of this cycle? Dating women you don't care about and then breaking up with them as soon as they get attached to you?"

For a moment Gio was back in Kane's house in upstate New York. He and Kane had become fast friends in middle school, and their friendship has survived eighteen years and Kane's inquisitive sister. "I thought you didn't like her. Want me to call her, give it another shot?"

Rena rolled her eyes and shuddered. "No. I'm pretty sure she's a vampire. All that pasty white skin, perfect makeup, and cold hands. I know she's the face of Umi Cosmetics, but they should let her eat something now and then. Maybe she'd smile."

Against his will, Gio chuckled. "She wasn't that bad."

"Not to you."

Losing some patience with the topic, Gio said, "I'll call her. She knows the score, though. I never lied to her."

"Lied to who?" Nick Andrade, Gio's very silent business partner and younger brother, asked as he sauntered into the office in his custom gray Corneliani suit that had never seen the inside of a boardroom. "You broke it off with Miss Cosmetics already? Damn. I'm going to miss her. She was gorgeous."

Rena made a sound of disgust deep in her chest. "I don't

know which one of you is worse."

Nick smiled suggestively and wiggled his eyebrows in the disarming manner that won him more female attention than was good for him. "That's because you won't give me a chance to show you how good I really am."

"It's a struggle, but I take it one day at a time." Rena rolled her eyes dramatically. Gio would have told Nick to back off, but the two of them had bantered like that for as long as he could remember. And Nick was smart enough to know that if he ever actually made a play for Rena he wouldn't live long. Either Gio or Kane would put a quick end to it.

Nick's eyes narrowed. "Luckily, I didn't come here for you. I came to see Gio."

Years of frustration with his brother's disinterest in the family company surfaced as a barb. "Putting in your one day of work this year? It's only September."

Plopping down in a chair in front of Gio, Nick propped his feet up on the leather antique chair across from him. "I may come to work every day now. I don't know what I did to deserve it, but I love it, Gio."

Gio reached down and shoved his brother's feet to the floor. "What the hell are you talking about?"

"The Barbie doll of a chauffer you hired for me. She can drive me anywhere. She thought I wanted to come here, and I didn't have the heart to tell her no, so here I am." His smile grew wider. "Then I met my swimsuit model of a secretary and I knew it couldn't be an accident. What do you want, Gio? I'm in. Just tell me I can keep them."

Gio looked across at Rena and frowned. "Get rid of them."

Rena turned on Nick. "I hope you're happy. Two very nice women are about to lose their jobs. Why? Because—"

Nick's expression darkened. "Because my brother has no sense of humor."

Gio sighed. "You don't have to fire them. Transfer them."

She nodded, glared at Nick one final time, and left.

Nick stood. "You're always in a bad mood, so this is probably a ridiculous question—but did something happen I should know about?"

The question hit too close to the truth. In no conceivable scenario would he discuss what was bothering him with his brother, so he chose a topic that needed addressing. "I didn't close the Westport deal."

"No?" Nick's surprise was genuine. Then he relaxed and said, "I'm sure it's only a matter of time. You always get what you want."

Gio returned to his desk and sat. "Not always. I can't seem to keep you out of the papers."

Nick shrugged. "She said they were separated. Her husband only leaked the story because he was caught getting his own on the side. Does it really matter?"

"Her husband is an old buddy of one of the bidders for the land lease. He outbid me, just to screw with us. So, yes, it matters. I don't care if you never sit in a board meeting or answer one goddamn email I send you. You make sure your personal life does not affect this business. Are we clear?"

Nick's face reddened with anger. "Crystal. Cogent is all that really matters. It's all that ever has."

As the two brothers faced off, Gio glimpsed the past in his brother's eyes. Nick never understood the decisions Gio had made for the family. He likely never would.

Nick stood at the door as if he wanted to say something more, then turned and strode out the office.

Gio let out a long breath. As children, he and Nick had dreamed of running the family business together. Only two years apart, they'd once been close. He didn't normally waste time regretting the part he'd played in changing that.

The past was where it belonged.

Dead and gone.

A light knock on the door broke his thoughts.

"Miss Bennett is here to see you."

ଔ

A few moments earlier, as she'd entered the Cogent Building, Julia had smoothed her hands down the tan slacks of her security uniform and struggled to come up with an excuse for her behavior the night before. Her hair was neatly braided. Her makeup was minimal. Hopefully Mr. Andrade would understand that she hadn't been herself last night.

What do you say to a man you assaulted with a lamp the night before?

You look well, Mr. Andrade.

No, he'll think I'm being sarcastic.

Sorry, sir. It was either clock you with a lamp or wrestle you to the floor, and I was afraid I'd enjoy the latter too much.

No. No. No.

Honesty is not always the best policy.

A small smile pulled at her lips as she remembered how tempted she'd been to run her hands up those fabulous abs and kiss the arrogance right out of him. She shook her head. Grabbing the lamp in a desperate move, born in the confusion of unexpected passion, was not likely the best excuse to use either.

It was a matter of hit you or hit on you, sir.

Yeah, that's not going to work.

I'm screwed.

Maybe I'm worrying for nothing. He won't want to see me. CEOs don't handle this kind of thing themselves. He probably spoke to Paul's supervisor.

I'll get a written reprimand.

Maybe a verbal one, too.

I hope I didn't get Paul in too much trouble.

Breathe.

I'll make it right. I'll write up my report first thing and submit it. The whole thing was my fault. I'll make that clear.

As she stepped farther into the foyer, she stopped midstep. Two new security guards sat in Paul and Tom's seats. They were dressed in the same uniforms, but neither smiled as she approached their desk. One of them walked out from behind their station and stood at military-like attention in front of her. "Mr. Andrade requested that you report to his office as soon as you arrive."

He wants to see me.

Oh, my God, he wants to see me.

Don't get excited. This isn't a good thing.

"I should put my bag in the monitor room," Julia hedged and took a side step in that direction. *While I figure out what I'm going to say. And get this smile off my face or he'll never believe that I'm sorry about last night.*

The guard stepped in front of her and blocked her way. "We have coverage in there already," he said, looking past her as if dismissing her.

Coverage? The word was an unwelcome dose of reality.

Because I hit him, not because he spent the night, as I did, imagining what would have happened between us if I hadn't.

"Am I fired? Where are Paul and Tom?" Julia demanded as her agitation grew.

She might as well have asked two stone statues, for all their expressions gave away. The stoic wall of muscle merely repeated, "Please report to Mr. Andrade's office."

Julia looked back and forth between the two men, then asked, in a confidential tone, "Would you tell me if the police were up there? Blink twice fast if they are."

Neither man reacted at all.

Nothing.

Fine.

I can't be arrested for hitting someone I thought was an intruder.

Hopefully.

Head held high, she strode to the elevator with purpose. It was only once she was inside that she hugged her arms around her waist for a moment and let out a nervous breath.

How you respond to adversity determines the level of success you will achieve. She quoted the chapter heading from one of the books she'd been reading, using the words to calm herself. None of the books, however, soothed the gnawing feeling in her gut—because she was more nervous about how her body would respond to her boss than afraid he'd fire her.

Maybe I'll get in there and realize that I'm not attracted to him at all. I was excited about meeting with a buyer. My adrenaline was probably running high. I'll see him again, feel nothing, and have something to laugh about with my friends when I go home.

Stepping out of the elevator, she headed into Mr. Andrade's outer office and faced her fear. *Or I'll make a complete fool of myself by staring longingly at him while he tries to explain why I'm no longer employed here—or worse, has me hauled off in cuffs.*

Her heart was beating so loudly in her ears she didn't actually hear if Mr. Andrade's secretary said, "Wait while I announce you," or "Follow me, please." Julia stood frozen near Rena's desk.

Rena held the door to her boss's office open, said something to the man waiting inside, then turned back to Julia and said, "Are you ready?"

Yes.

No.

"Is he alone?" Julia asked, hating that her voice sounded nervous.

"Yes," Rena said and waved her forward.

Forcing her reluctant feet toward the open office door, Julia sought one last reassurance. "Does he look angry?"

With a sympathetic smile, Rena peeked in at her boss, gave Julia a conspiratorial wink, and whispered, "Always. But he's all growl and no bite. If he yells at you, just cry. He can't handle that."

Julia found herself smiling back at the woman she'd spoken to only once before as they'd shared a coffee break in the downstairs café.

Want to be a shark? Swim with the sharks.
I should write to that author and have him add:
Want to survive meeting a shark?
Be nice to his secretary.

Julia mouthed, "Thank you," as she walked past Rena, then tried not to turn and bolt as the door closed behind her. She forced herself to walk across the room until she was just a few feet in front of Mr. Andrade's desk. When she couldn't put off the inevitable any longer, she raised her eyes from the carpeting and met his.

Wham.

There it was.

From the nervous flutter in her stomach to her wildly thudding heart, there was no denying the intensity of the attraction. He held her eyes, stood, and approached her.

The air between them sizzled, and she knew in that moment he felt it, too; that indescribable pull that defies logic.

Everything Julia had thought she'd say flew out of her head. She stood, immobile, barely breathing as he closed the distance between them. She licked her bottom lip nervously, and his eyes locked to that movement before returning to hers.

He didn't look happy, but he did look... hungry. He bent so close to her that if she went on her tiptoes their lips would meet. He hovered, as if he, too, were testing what neither of them could deny.

Down, libido. There are reasons why this man is off limits.
Good reasons.

I can't think of any right this minute, but they will come to me.

The room around them disappeared. Everything beyond him faded into the background—insignificant when compared to how he made her feel. *Is this the zing people speak of?*

"Did you make your date last night, Miss Bennett?" he asked.

Julia swallowed nervously. "It wasn't a date. Well, it shouldn't have been a date. It was supposed to be a business opportunity, but..." She let her words trail off as she realized she was rambling. She cleared her throat. "Yes, I made it there on time."

"I'm relieved to hear it. I'd hate to think that your job here impeded your social time."

"It doesn't," she said quickly before she realized he was being sarcastic. Since she'd only worked for her parents, Julia wasn't used to having a boss. She didn't hide her irritation with him. "I was scheduled to leave early."

He studied her for a moment, then said, "You didn't recognize the CEO of the company you work security for. And then you attacked me." He touched his bruised temple. "Give me one good reason why I shouldn't fire you."

His brusque tone increased Julia's nervousness. She reminded herself what his secretary had said: He's all growl and no bite. *I wonder if he's the same in bed, because that would be a shame. A nip from him might be nice.* She bit her lip and chastised herself. *Stop that. This is serious.* In desperation, she said the first repeatable thing that came into her head. "Because I've proven that I'm serious about defending your office?"

He frowned. "Do you find this situation amusing, Miss Bennett?"

No, just my reaction to you. Julia lowered her eyes and remembered how he'd looked in his workout clothes. She'd thought he looked sexy in those, but he also looked amazing in a suit. *I bet he's one of those lucky few people who also look good naked. Not everyone can pull that off, but I bet he does.* "No, Mr. Andrade."

"Do you believe that you're suited for your job?"

Julia look up and met his eyes. "It's not hard. It's just watching the monitors. Nothing happens at night so it gives me plenty of time to read."

He cocked his head to one side and narrowed his eyes. "While you're working?"

She played her comment back in her head and groaned. "That didn't come out right. Of course I don't read in the surveillance room. If I did, I wouldn't be watching the monitors, would I? And I watch them. Very closely. All night." She rounded her eyes innocently for emphasis.

He leaned in and looked as if he was about to say something, then changed his mind. "That's all, Miss Bennett."

Unsure of what that meant, Julia didn't move. "I'm sorry?"

"You can go now."

She turned to leave, then turned back and asked, "Do I still work here?"

He covered his eyes with one hand and rubbed them as if her question caused him pain. "Yes."

Not giving him time to change his mind, Julia fled from his office. As she rushed by Rena's desk, the secretary asked, "So, how did it go?"

"Hard to say," Julia said and kept walking. *As long as he can't read minds I'm in the clear.*

Chapter Four

GIO FOUGHT AND won against the desire to call her back in. *I shouldn't have brought her up here in the first place. I should have called the head of security and let him deal with it.*

But I had to see her again.

He'd wanted to reassure his cock that she was nothing special. *See, just another woman.* Unfortunately, for reasons he couldn't explain, she was more than that. When she spoke he had a difficult time concentrating on anything beyond how she would cry out in that sweet voice, begging him to go deeper, while he pounded into her.

Around her, he felt dangerously impulsive, and that was completely uncharacteristic of him. In his family, he was the reliable one. He had taken over Cogent Solutions after his father's death because he'd been the natural choice, not because it was something he wanted. No one had debated the decision or asked how he felt about it. He hadn't even asked himself.

Family was about duty—sustaining and protecting it.

Decisively.

Orderly.

The women he dated understood that he didn't want more than a casual, sexual relationship. They didn't ask questions, they didn't sleep over, and when it was over they moved on to another wealthy man. No hard feelings. No complications. Jealousy was for men who couldn't find another woman, and that had never been a problem for Gio.

He was generous with the women he dated. He gave them enough jewelry to make even the most jaded of them smile. He took them to the posh places wealthy people went when they wanted to be seen. The society pages in almost any city he visited ran photos of him with whomever he was dating. To many of these women, their representation in the media was more important than what happened behind closed doors. It was a reality of his world and something he accepted.

The papers called him one of Manhattan's most eligible bachelors. His friends called him lucky. He didn't feel one way or another about either title.

In private affairs as well as in business, the one with the clear head won. Emotions were a distraction. They led to chaos and poor decisions.

Speaking of chaos.

He touched the small mark on his temple and smiled.

What is wrong with me? Instead of firing her, I just stood there imagining what it would be like to bend her over the back of that couch and claim her as mine. His half-cocked erection was an uncomfortable reminder of the intensity of his attraction to her.

She's off limits.

She works for me, for God's sake.

Forget her.

Gio walked back to his desk and tossed Julia Bennett's folder on top of the others. He threw himself into work for the next several hours, only checking his watch when he noticed the sun had gone down. Nine o'clock. He stood and stretched.

Rena would be long gone. *Thank God.* He didn't want to discuss anything from the night before with her.

He called downstairs to have his car brought around to the front. He often left the building through the lower garage, but tonight he decided to leave through the front foyer. He paused in front of the security station. The two temporary security guards looked fresh from military training. They stood as soon as they saw him exit the elevator.

He nodded to them and couldn't help scanning the area behind them. One of the doors behind them led to the surveillance room, but he wasn't sure which one. Julia Bennett was back there somewhere.

Reading, probably.

He shook his head ruefully.

He should be irritated by that knowledge, but instead he wondered what topics held her interest. He forced himself to walk away, even though, he admitted, he really wanted to find her and ask her.

Ridiculous.

ᘓ

Julia sighed audibly as she watched Gio Andrade leave the building on one of the monitors. He probably always walked through the foyer, but she let herself imagine he'd done it because he'd wanted to see her again.

There is nothing wrong with a healthy fantasy life, as long as you don't act upon it. Julia chuckled. She felt like she was back in high school, suffering from her first big crush. The difference was, no crush had ever made her feel quite so much like ripping her clothing off.

Maybe my menstrual cycle is going haywire. She'd read a study done on women during different times of the month. During ovulation, they were attracted to strong, aggressive men. The narrator had claimed this was due to an instinct to mate with the hardiest of the breed. Later in the month, women would find nicer, softer men attractive. *No, I'm pretty sure I'd think he's hot every day of the month.*

Her usual motivational reading material was put aside for the night. Instead, she used her phone to do an Internet search on the man she couldn't get out of her head. Interestingly enough, there were very few articles of substance on him. Almost every article had featured him with a new woman on his arm. Gio taking an heiress to the ballet. Gio and a movie star at a fundraiser. The cameras loved him. No matter how hard she searched, she'd yet to come up with an embarrassing photo, or anything that mentioned how he'd made his money.

Why am I wasting my time reading about a man who has certainly already forgotten about me? She closed her eyes, hoping it would help clear her head, but he was just as vivid in her imagination:

I can see it now. He'd crash the door of my office open and say, "Miss Bennett."

Julia rested her head on her hands, letting the fantasy come to life. In her mind, her voice was sexily husky. *"You shouldn't be here, Mr. Andrade."*

He'd loosen his tie and throw it on the floor. Julia rewound the moment in her head. *No, he'd toss it on the back of the chair. That's an expensive coat.*

"Call me Gio. Practice saying it, because you'll be screaming it all night."

Would he be that crass?

Julia started their conversation over.

"You shouldn't be here, Mr. Andrade."

He'd walk over and hold out a hand to me. "I couldn't stay away from you."

I'd take his hand and stand before him. "You know this is wrong."

"How could it be when it feels this good?"

She imagined his lips on hers and smiled. *He would definitely know how to kiss. I'd try to remain strong. I'd push him back, playfully protesting. "What about all those other women?"*

"They mean nothing to me. They never have. You're the only one who—"

The phone on her desk rang, cutting off whatever Dream Gio would have said. She opened her eyes and answered the landline. The super-serious replacement security guard said, "Mr. Andrade has left the building. The cleaning staff is also gone for the night. That should be everyone. Have you seen any stragglers?"

Julia sat up and straightened her shirt. "No," she said. "I haven't seen anyone." She moved her purse completely off the desk so it was no longer blocking one of the screens. "But you'll be the first to hear if I do."

The security guard hung up without further comment.

Julia leaned back in her chair and looked at the ceiling. *Stop daydreaming. Focus on what's important and be grateful you still have a job.*

Remember why you're in New York.

Julia leaned down and pulled a magazine out of her purse. She flipped to the article that had inspired her purchase: "Visualizing Your Way to the Top."

A flash of how Gio would look beneath her, grinding upward into her while she threw her head back in abandon, warmed her cheeks. *I have no problem visualizing it at all. That's the problem.*

Julia dropped the magazine back into her bag and tried to focus on the monitors. Nothing unusual, but that was no surprise. She rubbed her tired eyes. Only five more hours until her shift was over.

It's going to be a long night.

Chapter Five

THE NEXT EVENING Julia let out a sigh of relief at seeing familiar faces sitting at the security desk. She walked over to the front of their station and said, "You both look like you're feeling better. I'm glad you're back. Paul, I am so sorry about the other night."

Slightly older than Paul, Tom was the veteran on their security team and almost always a voice of reason. "It's hard to believe either of you are still employed here. Can't I take a day off without all hell breaking loose?"

Paul shrugged and smiled sheepishly. "Hey, I was sick. If you'd been here, I wouldn't have had to ask Julia to cover the desk, but you took the night off."

The two men bickered more like brothers than coworkers.

Julia was moved to voice her apology again. "Paul, I feel awful about—"

He waved her concern off. "Eh, don't worry. I got a warning and a note in my file. Nothing big. How about you? Everyone has been tight-lipped about you actually attacking Mr. Andrade. What did you get?"

Close enough to him that my nights have been filled with spicy dreams about him? Julia choked that honest answer back. "The same. I'm just glad it blew over." Julia hitched her purse on her shoulder and said, "I guess I should get back there."

Paul interrupted. "Hey, you didn't say what happened with your jewelry guy."

Tom said, "Paul, don't make her say it. She would have told us if she had good news."

"Just because you're married now doesn't mean you suddenly have deeper insights into everyone with a vagina. Julia and I are friends. Don't tell me how to talk to her."

"First, I don't know a man who uses the word 'vagina.' Never say it again. Second, unlike you, I have sisters. You can make a woman cry if you bring up something she failed at. They're sensitive."

"How do you know she failed? She may have nailed it." Paul turned to Julia. "What happened?"

She covered her eyes with one hand and groaned.

Tom said, "See now you've upset her. I told you to drop it."

"Stop telling me what to do."

"Someone has to. You have the social skills of a gorilla and the vocabulary of an adolescent."

"Vagina. Vagina. Vagina."

"That's really mature."

The banter of the two overly muscled security guards pulled Julia back from her inner pity party. She lowered her hand and half smiled. "Paul, you were right. The skirt was too short. He wasn't interested in buying my jewelry. A total creep. And he was married."

Paul was on his feet in a heartbeat. "Did he touch you? You tell me where he lives and I'll break his legs."

Tom frowned and said, "I can't help Paul. My wife would kill me. But I know someone who does that kind of thing cheap."

There was something wonderfully reassuring about their support, even if it was a little extreme. "It's fine, guys. I should have known something was up when he didn't want to meet me where he worked. He probably isn't even a buyer. I have a lot to learn about living in the city."

Paul came around the podium and gave her a hug. "You're a beautiful woman, Julia. Guys can't help but want to fuck you."

Julia pulled back at his words and burst out laughing. Although many women would have found Paul physically attractive, Julia had never viewed him as a romantic possibility.

He said whatever came to his mind. Julia had gotten used to his candor, but she couldn't take him seriously.

He stepped back, seeming to be shocked by his own admission. Then he smiled and shrugged. "I didn't mean that the way it sounded."

Tom said, "Get over here, Paul. You went too far. You were doing fine... and then you had to cross the line. That's why you're still single. It's your mouth. And, Julia, stay away from Paul. He has a hard enough time concentrating without you as a distraction."

Julia and Paul stood there for a moment longer, smiling guiltily like children who'd just been lectured. Over the last month, the three of them had gotten into this playful cycle of ribbing each other. It was harmless and started all of their days with a smile.

Still laughing, Julia turned to head to the surveillance room and crashed into a much more refined wall of muscle. One that sent a sledgehammer of heat through her. She raised her eyes slowly, shuddering with pleasure as his two strong hands steadied her. If the dark expression on his face was anything to go by, he was not as happy to see her. Barely above a whisper, she said, "Mr. Andrade."

"Miss Bennett," he said curtly, but his hands remained on her arms. "I'd like to speak with you for a moment."

Julia looked back at Paul and Tom and grimaced. "I'll be right back."

Gio put a hand forcibly on Julia's lower back and guided her to the first floor café, which was busy in the mornings but in the evenings was closed and deserted. Once inside, they stood facing each other, so closely that Julia was sure he'd be able to hear what his nearness was doing to her heartbeat.

"Cogent Solutions has a strict no-dating policy among coworkers. That includes the members of my security team," he said harshly.

So much for how I imagined this conversation would go. Julia blushed and pointed in the direction of the security desk.

She hoped he hadn't heard what Paul had said to her. "We were just kidding around. It's harmless."

He leaned a little closer and Julia quickly looked down, afraid her eyes would reveal how he was making her feel.

"You should be more careful, Miss Bennett. A man could get the wrong impression about you."

Her eyes flew up to clash with his. "I appreciate your concern, Mr. Andrade, but it's unnecessary. I get along well with both Tom and Paul. We sometimes laugh. It's what people do when they work together."

"I don't like him near you." His eyes burned into hers.

Her breath caught in her throat. She shook her head, sure that she had misunderstood what she'd heard. "I'm sorry?"

He brushed a thumb softly across her lower lip. "You heard me." He dropped his hand, spun on his heel, and walked away.

Julia stood rooted to the spot until Gio was out of sight. She sank down into one of the wooden chairs and let out a shaky breath.

I heard you.

I just wish I hadn't.

It was one thing to fantasize about him. That was harmless. It was completely different and even scary to consider for a moment that he might be attracted to her. *Men like him don't date women like me.*

He might try to for a one-night stand.

Maybe he considered it amusing to step outside his usual diet of models to flirt with a regular woman, but in no one's universe was it a good idea to even consider getting involved with him.

I should have told him I have a boyfriend.

I should have told him it wasn't appropriate to talk to me like that. But what did I do? I just stood there staring at him like some easy mark. No wonder he thinks I'm interested. I make a complete fool out of myself every time I see him.

I can't hide in here forever.

Julia stood and straightened her shoulders with determination. *Nothing happened. Nothing is going to happen. For all I know, he was teasing me. Maybe he has a sick sense of humor.* She shook it off and walked past Tom and Paul, hoping they wouldn't ask her what the great Mr. Andrade had wanted.

Tom pushed his chair back and stood at her approach. "Julia and the boss? When were you going to tell me about this?"

Paul defended himself. "I didn't know. The last time I saw the two of them she was trying to kill him with a lamp."

"This is not good. You have to talk to her."

"Me? You're the one who is so great with women."

Julia broke into their stage-whispered conversation. "I'm fine, Guys. It's not what you're thinking."

With a shake of his head, Tom sat back down. "You're an awful liar, Julia. I've never seen Mr. Andrade do anything inappropriate, but it's obvious he's interested in you. Avoid him. I don't want to see you get hurt.

Julia nodded, rushed to the privacy of her monitor room, closed the door, leaned back, and closed her eyes. Was it possible that Tom was right?

Was Gio seriously interested in her?

And if he was, how was she going to find the strength to avoid him?

By reminding myself that getting involved with him will only lead to heartache? That it would be a distraction I don't need right now?

Julia sank back into the chair behind the monitors and laid her forehead down on her folded hands.

If I know all of that, why can't I get this stupid smile off my face?

ଔ

Gio paced his home office in his Upper West Side penthouse apartment. He'd brought work home with him, but it was still tucked, untouched, in his briefcase. Although he notoriously worked late, he'd thought a different location would help clear his head.

So far, it wasn't helping.

He couldn't concentrate. He groaned as he remembered what he'd said to Julia in the café. She brought out a possessive side of him he hadn't known he had. He'd wanted to rip her away from the security guards when he'd seen her laughing with them.

He told himself to keep walking. It was none of his business who she spoke to, who she laughed with, unless it affected her job performance. Even then, he wouldn't normally have wasted his time by getting involved. He would've mentioned it to Rena and she would've sent an email to the head of the security department.

He had never imagined himself as the type of man who would proclaim he was uncomfortable with any woman's relationship with her coworkers; like some jealous boyfriend.

And that's what made Julia dangerous.

He wasn't himself around her.

I should just fuck her and get it over with.

Nothing breeds contempt better than familiarity. By trying to deny whatever this is, I'm giving it an artificial importance.

For all I know she lives with someone. She may have dated half the men at Cogent while I was away. That possibility alone should be enough to keep me away from her. Getting involved with Julia could get complicated. He didn't do complicated.

He opened the doors to his balcony and stepped outside, hoping the fresh air would return some of his sanity. As he looked over the skyline of the city, he wondered if what he felt for Julia was merely a side effect of how he'd been feeling lately.

A few months ago, if someone had asked him how he felt about his life he would have said he was comfortable with where he was and what he was doing. His business was thriving. Any drama that had existed within his family was in the distant past. His social life was full, even if it was unexciting when compared to his brother Nick's.

Unfortunately he had made the mistake of attending a summer function with the side of his family he normally avoided. Seeing his uncles again had rekindled memories of betrayal. And, much like with Julia, he didn't like how those old emotions threatened the calm he had worked so hard to achieve.

Every time Madison Andrade contacted him, he was reminded of how fake that side of the family was. His uncles often spoke of love and family loyalty, but when he and his brothers had needed them the most, they had proven how hypocritical and self-serving they were. He wouldn't be fooled by them twice.

Maybe it's time for me to take a page out of my brother's book and do something I want to do.

Or, rather, someone I want to do.

A little complication might be just the distraction I'm looking for.

Chapter Six

A FEW DAYS later, Julia checked the messages on her phone from the window seat on a public bus. She wasn't worried about missing her stop since she knew the route well. This was a ride she took as many days as she could. Down to the Diamond District with her bag that doubled as a display case for her jewelry.

Her phone rang.

"Julia." Her father's ever-cheerful voice rang clear across the miles. "What are you up to today?"

She smiled into the phone. "The usual. I try to pitch to one new jewelry store each day."

"You must be a pro by now."

"Or something," she said with some irony. She didn't know if she was getting better at pitching her jewelry, but she was definitely becoming more experienced doing it.

"I am so proud of you."

"Thanks, Dad. Eventually one of the stores is going to buy my line. Or, I will have the dubious title of being one of the few people who has met every single jeweler in New York City."

"Just be yourself, Julia. That's the best sales pitch."

"I'm not sure I should take advice from someone Mom used to hide from customers."

"That's only because when they asked me for my opinion I would give them my honest answer. Your mother is much more diplomatic than I am."

"How is she?"

Her father was quiet for a moment. "She had a good day yesterday. I took her to the ocean. Do you remember the beach she always took you to when you were little? The one with the abandoned stone building next to it? You used to picnic in front of it. Then you always begged her to take you inside. She'd tell you that it wasn't a good idea, but the two of you would go in anyway. She told me it was your fault. You used to pretend you knew the last owners and would insist that you'd promised you would take care of their old place. Your mother always did have a weak spot for dreamers."

"She told you that yesterday?"

"No, honey, she didn't remember the place."

Julia bit her lip and looked sadly down at her lap. For just a moment, she had let herself believe in what she knew was impossible. "I thought you said she was doing much better on her new medication."

Her father's tone was gentle. "She is. We had a good day together. That's what's important right now. She's happy. That's all I care about. I want that for you too, Julia. Whether it's in New York or here with us... whether you sell every piece of jewelry you make, or you discover you want something else entirely, it doesn't matter. Just find something that makes you happy."

The bus began to fill and a woman sat down in the seat next to Julia. The glare the woman gave her was a not-so-subtle hint to end the call. "I have to go, Dad. I'll call you tomorrow."

Julia was about to return her phone to her purse when it rang again. "Did you forget something?" she asked with a laugh.

"Julia," a familiar male voice said, sending instant shivers of desire through her.

"Mr. Andrade?"

"Call me Gio. I need to see you tonight."

"About my job?"

"No," he said simply, and Julia felt her face warm with embarrassment.

"I work the overnight shift," she said and turned her face toward the window of the bus.

"I'm sure your boss will understand if you call in sick."

Julia chewed her bottom lip, then said, "This isn't a good idea."

"No, it's a very, very bad idea, but one I hope you find as irresistible as I do. Say yes, Julia."

And there it was—confirmation of the desire she thought she'd seen in his eyes. Her body clamored in response to the knowledge that their attraction was mutual. Perhaps because she was fresh from speaking with her family, but his offer— although tempting—was one that she knew she had to refuse. "I can't." She grasped at a reason. "I don't like to call in. I would feel too guilty to enjoy myself."

"Tomorrow night then."

"I'm scheduled every night straight through the weekend."

Impatiently, Gio said, "Am I missing something? Your file said you were single."

Irked by his assumption that she should jump at an invitation from him, Julia said, "Is it inconceivable that a woman would say no to you, Mr. Andrade?"

"This isn't about any woman. It's about you."

Julia swallowed hard. *This is real. How easy would it be to say yes to him? To temporarily forget about why I'm in New York City? To throw caution to the wind just this once?*

Then what?

He rarely dated a woman long enough to be photographed with her more than once.

I don't want to be just another name on some rich man's list of conquests. "Considering the women you're usually seen with, I'm flattered. But my answer is no, Mr. Andrade."

Julia hung up the phone and held it against her chest.

The woman next to her looked over and asked, "Married man?"

Julia shook her head.

"Old and ugly?"

Julia smiled. "He's actually gorgeous."

"Then you are a fool, honey. It's hard to find a man in the city."

The bus pulled over to her stop. Julia stood, squeezed past everyone, and exited the bus with a sigh of relief. *I'm glad I said no. Even if he were the last single man in New York City, it wouldn't matter because I didn't come here to find a man. There will be plenty of time for all of that after I sell my jewelry line.*

I can find a nice guy back in Rhode Island. Someone who will love me the way my father loves my mother. Unconditionally. And through the good as well as the bad times.

Anything less than that is a waste of my time.

You keep telling yourself that, Julia.

You might even begin to believe it.

☙

A week later, Gio sat at the desk in his office, drumming the fingers of one hand on Julia's file. He'd asked her out and she'd refused. That should've been the end of it. Honestly, he should have been grateful she'd turned him down. Calling her had been a mistake. Actually sleeping with her would have been an even bigger one.

He'd tried to get her out of his head.

He'd called a well-known Broadway actress who had slipped him her number a few months ago while he'd been on a date with someone else. At the time he'd thought she was stunningly beautiful. However, only two minutes in the phone call, he'd realized he no longer had any interest in her.

A week of ignoring the problem hadn't made it go away.

There was only one woman he wanted.

One woman who was killing his ability to enjoy all others.

Julia.

"Rena, please have Julia Bennett come to my office as soon as she arrives tonight."

"Regarding a security concern, Gio? Gerry may still be in his office. Would you like me to call down and check?"

"No, that won't be necessary. Just send up Miss Bennett."

Rena was quiet for a moment, a telltale sign that she wanted to ask him about it. Finally, she replied, "Okay."

Anticipation built within Gio as he waited for Julia. He had to see her again. He had to know if he'd completely misread the signals from her.

What if she is as uninterested as she claims to be?

Did I only see what I wanted to see?

No, I didn't imagine anything. She may have reasons why she thinks she doesn't want to be with me, but it's not because she isn't attracted. I saw the way she looked at me.

There was a light knock on the door. "Gio, Miss Bennett is here to see you."

"Send her in," Gio said, hoping he didn't sound as excited as he felt about the prospect.

Dressed in her tan security uniform, Julia stepped into his office.

Rena hovered near the door.

"That'll be all, Rena," Gio said.

With obvious reluctance, Rena closed the door.

"You wanted to see me, Mr. Andrade?" Julia asked, sounding more than a little apprehensive about it.

"Come here, Julia."

Her eyes widened and she didn't move.

He walked toward her. He stopped just a few inches from her. Close enough that he could feel her breath become more erratic. "I told myself to leave you alone, but I can't stop thinking about you." He ran the back of his hand down one of her cheeks and heard her catch her breath.

 C3

Julia jumped as the door behind them crashed open and a tiny, visibly pregnant woman entered with Rena at her heels.

Visibly agitated, Rena said, "I'm so sorry, Gio, I told her you were in a meeting. She wouldn't wait."

The little brunette braced herself with one hand on her lower back. "I wouldn't be here if you were answering any of my calls."

Oh, my God. Tell me this isn't what I think it is.

"I'll handle this, Rena," Gio said and turned away from Julia to address the woman whom Julia prayed was not carrying his child.

Although, really, maybe it's for the best.

I was beginning to waver there.

So, thank you, nameless pregnant lady.

"I should go," Julia said and edged toward the door.

Gio pinned her with his hot gaze. *Oh, no, you cannot give me that look while fending off someone you knocked up. I'm outta here.*

"This will only take a moment," Gio said and turned his attention back to the other woman. They stood in front of the now-closed door, effectively blocking Julia's exit. "You shouldn't have come here, Madison."

"I had to."

Awkward.

"I've tried to be kind about it, but now I'll be blunt. Stop calling me. I'm not interested."

Oh, my God. I guess I knew that someone who dated so many people would be jaded, but he's a complete asshole.

"If you don't come, your brothers might back out, also."

What?

Okay, now I'm officially lost. This fight needs CliffsNotes.

"I won't take no for an answer, Gio. This is too important."

"It's a wedding. They'll survive my absence."

"Stephan wants the whole family there."

"I've seen Stephan once in the last five years. I don't really care what he wants."

"Then do it for me."

Oh, pumpkin, he is so close to telling you that he doesn't care about you either. Why would you do that to yourself? The petite woman shook her head sadly. "Whatever anger you're holding on to, let it go for one day." She rested a hand on her stomach and said, "The next generation will look to us for guidance about what it means to be a family. We are family, Gio, even if you don't want us to be."

The more Julia looked at both of them, the more similarities she saw in their features. If this woman wasn't carrying Gio's child, who was she to him?

There was such pain in Gio's eyes, it threw Julia into an emotional tailspin. It was hard enough to stay away from him when she thought of him as nothing more than an insanely attractive man with the hots for her. If he kept looking at the woman next to him like she was ripping his heart out, she was a goner for sure. She held her breath and waited for Gio's answer.

"Your father understands why I won't attend. So does your uncle," Gio said coldly, his tone not reflecting the hurt in his eyes.

The little brunette's eyes misted over and Julia felt hers do the same. She had no idea what was keeping their families apart, but she would have given anything to help them through something that was obviously tearing at both of them.

"No, they don't. They love you. You have no idea how happy they were to see you at Alethea's engagement party."

"I've given you the only answer you'll get from me. Now, please. Go."

Wiping away a stray tear, Madison put her hand on the door to open it. "I don't know why you're so angry, Gio."

"Then you're the lucky one in this," Gio said in an icy tone.

Looking somewhat deflated, Madison opened the door and left.

Whatever attraction Julia had felt for Gio was overshadowed by the emotion of the moment. She thought of her own family and how desperately she missed them, and burst out, "You can't let her go like that."

Face tight with anger, Gio didn't look away from the door. "It's none of your concern."

"She's pregnant."

Turning some of the anger on Julia, Gio growled, "A condition that had no relevance in my decision."

Julia threw up both of her hands in the air. "No relevance? You just threw a crying, pregnant woman out of your office."

"Enough. I didn't bring you here for this."

As loving as her family was, they called a spade a spade without remorse or hesitation. She'd been raised to appreciate the value of an honest opinion, and New York wasn't going to change that. The air that had been heavy with anticipation and attraction now crackled with more volatile emotions. "You know what your problem is?"

His eyes narrowed and he waited.

"I bet people don't tell you when you're behaving badly." Julia shook her head. "That was wrong. You should call her and apologize. I don't know what went on with your family, but I can't believe it was her fault. You shouldn't take it out on her."

For a moment Gio said nothing. "Is that it?"

No. Julia thought of how much she missed being able to talk to her mother, and that feeling gave her the courage to voice her thoughts. "If you're lucky enough to have family that loves you enough to chase you and beg you to come to their wedding, you should go. She was right. Whatever you're holding onto, you could put it aside for one day."

"That's a lot of advice from someone who knows nothing about the situation." His eyes were lit with a fire she couldn't decipher.

She held his eyes and defended herself. "I know that at the end of the day, family is all that matters. You're right, though. I don't know your situation and I don't know you. Maybe you and I don't share the same definition of family."

Without looking away, he took out his cell phone. He punched in a number, then waited, neither of them moving while it rang. "Madison. I've changed my mind. I will be attending the wedding. No, I'm sure my brothers will have the information. Yes, put me down for two." After listening to response on the other end of the line, Gio ended the call and replaced his phone in his breast pocket.

A sense of triumph filled Julia, followed by a pang of jealousy as she wondered who he'd be taking to the event.

"The wedding is in two weeks. We'll fly out the day before it."

"Me?" Julia swayed. "Where is the wedding?"

"It's on an island off the coast of Italy. And, yes, you. You're the one who thought it was important that I attend."

Oh, no, no, no. "I—we can't do that."

"Because?"

Because Italy means flying somewhere together and I can barely keep my hands off you now. "Because I work for you?" she practically squeaked. "You have a no-dating policy."

"An easy enough problem to solve. You're fired."

"You can't fire me. I need this job."

"Then we have a problem, because I'm not going to the wedding without you." He walked over until he once again stood so close that all she had to do was lean forward ever so slightly to be flush against him. Tip her head up just a fraction to make their lips would touch. "What would it take to get you to come with me?" His words hung between them, their dual meaning raising the heat in the room. He ran a light finger down the curve of her cheek and caressed the outline of her lips.

Julia shook her head free and backed up. Cornered, she blurted, "I'm not that kind of woman."

A corner of his mouth curled in a smile that didn't reach his eyes. "What kind of woman are you?"

"The kind who is smart enough to know this is a bad idea. I want to say yes." She took another step back. Being near him had her body humming with a need that scared her. As it often did when she was nervous, her mouth got ahead of her brain. "I mean, look at you. Who wouldn't want to say yes?" She bumped into the table with the lamp from their first encounter, and those memories only agitated her more. "But if I sleep with you once, I'll sleep with you twice. And then I'll get attached to you. You'll want to move on to the next woman and I'll be all clingy. Trust me, it'll get awkward." She touched her lips and imagined his kiss. "I can't do this."

With that, she bolted out of the room.

Chapter Seven

GIO WATCHED JULIA spring away from him and surprised himself by smiling. He was done trying to talk himself out of wanting her. He felt more alive around her than he could ever remember feeling.

Let her run.

It'll only make having her that much sweeter.

And I will have her.

A bright red object near one of the chairs caught his attention. She'd left her purse. He picked up her bag and headed out of his office, choosing his strategy as he walked. He deposited the bag on his secretary's desk and said, "Rena, Julia Bennett's address is in a folder on my desk. I want you to send her this and something nice..."

"No." Rena sat back in her chair.

Even though their conversations sometimes crossed into personal territory, Rena never argued with him. She may not have always agreed with how he handled his personal life, or that he involved her in it, but she had never refused him before.

The world was absolutely off-kilter that day.

"I wasn't asking."

Rena folded her hands in her lap. "I am not getting involved in this one. You're making a mistake. She's not your type. I actually like her."

"Weren't you lecturing me earlier on finding someone nice?"

Shaking her head, Rena pushed the bag back across his desk at him. "That was before I saw your cousin storm out of your office in tears. You're not ready for a nice woman. I've spoken to Julia. She's as sweet and trusting as they come, and someone may teach her a harsh lesson because of it—but I won't help that happen."

Picking up her bag, Gio found himself in the rare position of defending his actions. "I was merely asking you to return this."

"No," Rena said with finality.

With heat rising up his neck, Gio said, "Then I'll return it myself." Heading down to the lobby, he passed several of his employees before he realized the second looks they were giving him were due to the purse he clutched in his right hand. The realization didn't slow his long strides down to the security desk.

"Where is she?" he demanded of the two men behind the security desk.

"Who, sir?" the older of the two asked.

"Julia Bennett. Is she still here?"

The guard looked uncomfortable as he said, "She just left. I have someone coming in to cover her shift."

Left? "Do you know where she went?"

"I saw her outside talking to a..." He checked his log and continued, "Mrs. D'Argenson. They left together in a limo."

Madison and Julia?

How could they know each other?

In his office, it certainly hadn't appeared that they were acquainted. He didn't like surprises. He strode back up to his office, still clutching Julia's purse in one hand. As he passed Rena's desk, she asked, "Couldn't find her?"

In response, Gio did something he had never done before: Fueled by all the frustration building inside him, he slammed the door of his office shut.

He cursed and threw Julia's purse in the corner of his office.

How many times have I told Nick to stay away from women in this building? This is the reason. It's a distraction. I have phone calls to make. Leads to follow up on.

He sat down at his desk again but, instead of reaching for any of the piles of papers that required his attention, he reopened Julia's file. He traced the edge of her headshot that was stapled to her application.

What did she say? If she sleeps with me once, she'd sleep with me twice.

He groaned.

I have a feeling twice will be just how we start our first night together.

He shifted uncomfortably in his seat as his cock sprang to life in agreement.

Julia Bennett. I know what I want. What is it that you want?

০৪

Real life needs a rewind button.

If given a redo, I would not go upstairs to close the door for Paul.

I would not repeatedly make an ass out of myself in front of Gio Andrade.

I would definitely not tell him that I was tempted to sleep with him.

As Julia hastily exited Cogent Solutions, she noticed a black stretch limo parked in front of it, with the pregnant woman, Madison, standing beside it. *Maybe she won't see me.*

Madison stepped away from the vehicle and walked quickly toward Julia. "Excuse me. Can I talk to you for a minute?"

Julia looked around, then answered, "Sure, I guess."

"Are you leaving?"

As fast as I can. Julia nodded.

"Would you like a ride?"

Julia hesitated. The desire to get as far away as possible was strong. "I was going to take the bus."

Madison stepped forward and took Julia lightly by the arm. "Please. I'll drop you anywhere, and we can talk on the way."

Curiosity warred with common sense. *Admit it, you're hoping she tells you more about your hot boss.*

The driver held the back door of the limo open and Julia slid inside it. *So, what if I am? It doesn't mean I'll do anything about it. Anyone would be curious after the scene I witnessed upstairs.*

Madison sat down next to her and the driver closed the door. A moment later, they pulled into traffic. Madison turned in her seat and held out her hand to Julia. "I should have introduced myself upstairs. I'm Maddy D'Argenson. Gio's cousin."

Julia took her hand. "I'm Julia Bennett. Night security."

Maddy smiled at the title and shook her hand warmly. "I wanted to thank you for whatever you said to Gio about going to the wedding."

"His decision had nothing to do with me."

"Really? Have you known him long?"

"I don't actually know him at all. I work for him." Julia referenced her outfit. The limo took a left turn and Julia said, "Shouldn't I tell the driver where I live?"

"I was hoping you'd come somewhere with me first. There is someone I'd like you to meet."

Julia looked out the window to assess where they were. *The Lincoln Center? Where are we going?* "This was a mistake. Do you mind pulling over?"

A line of disappointment creased the rich woman's forehead. "Please. I just want to talk."

"About what?" Julia asked slowly.

"Please?" Maddy leaned forward and asked, her heart in her eyes. "This is more important to me than I could ever attempt to explain. Just give me a few minutes then I'll drop you off wherever you'd like. I promise."

Julia was pretty sure she'd used a similar tone with her own family when she really wanted something. It was impossible to look into Maddy's sweetly expectant face and disappoint her. Julia looked down at her attire. "I'm not dressed for anywhere nice."

With a triumphant smile, Maddy said, "Don't worry. We're going to a friend's place."

The limo pulled up to the front of an exclusive high-rise apartment building. A doorman rushed out to greet them. The driver helped Madison out of the car, but Julia hesitated. It felt safe to go with her. *After all, how dangerous could a pregnant woman be?*

Maddy smiled at the doorman and greeted him by name, then asked, "Is Miss Corisi home?"

He returned her smile and said, "Yes. She'll be happy to see you."

Maddy led the way to an elevator and Julia followed her into it. Maddy inserted a key that freed the elevator to go all the way to the top floor.

Penthouse. Of course. Why would anyone live on any other floor?

A butler answered the door almost immediately upon their arrival. He led them into a marble foyer that was lined with mountains of gifts on either side. A tall, thin, dark-haired woman in a simple yellow sundress rushed in and hugged Maddy. She ushered them inside and waved an arm toward the gifts. "Excuse the mess. They're coming in faster than I know what to do with them. I can't believe it's two weeks away. Nothing is ready."

Maddy hugged her again. "Everything will be perfect. I know it." Remembering Julia, she reached back and pulled her forward. "I brought someone I want you to meet."

Julia awkwardly offered the woman her hand. "Hello." And then looked back at Maddy for guidance after she shook the woman's delicate hand.

Maddy laughed. "I'm sorry. I'm doing this badly. Julia, this is Nicole. Nicole Corisi." When Julia didn't react to the name, Maddy added, "Nicole is marrying my cousin, Stephan."

Julia smiled weakly. "Congratulations?"

Why am I here again?

Maddy was hopping beside her with excitement. "Nicole, Julia convinced Gio to come to your wedding."

Nicole cocked her head to the side and looked Julia over from head to toe. "Is she one of yours?"

Maddy shook her head. "No, but trust me. She's the one. You should have seen them together."

"It won't count," Nicole said with a smile.

"It doesn't matter," Maddy countered. "She's perfect for him."

The obscurity of the conversation was beginning to make Julia nervous. "Okay, it was nice meeting the two of you." She started backing toward the door they had entered through. "Thank you for the ride. I just remembered that I have somewhere I need to be."

"You can't leave," Maddy said quickly.

Nicole placed her hand on Maddy's arm to caution her. "We're scaring her. Julia, if this is your first experience with Maddy, let me just assure you that she is as harmless as she is crazy. The first ride I took in her limo ended with me delivering her baby. This can't be worse than that."

"I'm not scared," Julia lied. "You ladies seem wonderful, but I can't stay." She bumped into the butler as she backed up and almost fell, but he caught her and set her back on her feet. "I have to—"

"Aren't you curious why I brought you here?" Maddy asked.

Shaking her head, Julia stepped around the butler. "I'm really not a curious person in general. Really, most of the world is a mystery to me and I'm fine with that."

"She's funny," Nicole said with a growing smile. "I like her."

"I know, right?" Maddy said in agreement. She beat Julia to the door, blocking her exit. "Just hear us out."

With her escape effectively blocked by a pregnant woman, Julia braced herself. *Money makes people weird. Just smile. Agree. Eventually she'll step away from the door... then bolt.* "Okay."

"Would you like to come in and sit?"

Julia shrugged with what she hoped looked like confidence. "I'm fine here in the hall."

Her sweet smile returning, Maddy said, "Family is everything to me."

Okay, so crazy lady and I can agree on one point. Julia merely nodded.

"We almost lost Stephan this past summer, and it made us realize how short and fragile life can be. Stephan and I reached out to Gio and his brothers with the idea of mending ties with them. I didn't know until I met Gio that he was so angry with us. He said he wants nothing to do with us."

Nicole added drolly, "Some people would have taken that as a sign to leave him alone, but Maddy can't stand anyone being upset with her."

"It's not that, Nicole. He doesn't hate us. He's hurting." She looked across at Julia and said, "Sometimes the right woman can crack a man's heart wide open and bring him back from a dark place."

Julia leaned back against the wall in surprise. "You think I'm that woman? I barely know him. You misunderstood what you saw." The disappointment in Maddy's eyes was so genuine that Julia felt for her, despite the odd situation. "Instead of trying to set him up with someone, maybe you should kidnap *him*."

"Did I totally misread what I saw?" Tears came to Maddy's eyes. "I'm sorry. I'm so emotional lately." She laughed. "No wonder you think I'm crazy. Looking at the last hour through your eyes I can see why you'd be eager to get away from us. I just got so excited by the possibility. I can't help thinking that if he falls in love with someone nice he'll find his way back to us. When I saw the way he was looking down at you when I walked in, I thought... I don't know what I was thinking. Are you sure there is nothing between you?"

Against all common sense, Julia admitted, "He did ask me to go to the wedding."

Nicole exclaimed, "He did?"

Maddy's whole expression changed instantly and her smile returned. "I knew it. I knew he was into you."

"I turned him down."

Maddy clapped her hands together. "You are perfect." She turned to Nicole, beaming. "Come on, admit it. She is."

Nicole looked Julia over again and said, "It's a long shot. Even if they fall in love it doesn't mean you'll reach him. Not every story has a happy ending, Maddy. What if this doesn't work out and you end up making things worse?"

Maddy threw up her hands in the air and walked over to Nicole. "When are you going to trust me? I never fail."

Seizing the opportunity Maddy presented by moving away from the door, Julia threw it open and bolted down the stairs. She didn't stop until she was out the front entrance and a block away.

She hunched over, hands on her thighs, and tried to catch her breath.

New York, you are one strange city.

You're not scaring me off, but let's be honest: You could use a little therapy.

She stepped out into the street to hail a cab, then realized she didn't have her purse with her and swore.

Great.

Just great.

My money is in my purse. My cell phone. My keys.

And I left it... yep, in Gio Andrade's office.

Only... she checked the street signs... *fifteen blocks away.*

Just perfect.

Chapter Eight

HIS BREATH CAUGHT in his throat when he heard someone enter the outer office. He stood, then sat, then stood again and crossed the room decisively. Their eyes met and held with a heat he no longer tried to deny. "You left your purse," he said in a harsher tone than he'd intended.

She looked flustered, windblown, and utterly irresistible. "I realized that about fifteen blocks from here."

He took a step toward her, then stopped. The desire to continue toward her and pull her into his arms was strong, but he didn't want her to bolt again. "You could have called me. I would have sent a driver to pick you up."

She gave him a small, pained smile. "It's okay, it gave me time to think. Plus, I don't know your number. I don't know you at all."

He moved closer but stopped when she stepped back. "I intend to change that."

She shook her head. "No." She looked around the room until she saw her purse, then crossed the room to pick it up. When she met his eyes again, a new emotion darkened her expression.

He walked over and stood near her, so close their breath mingled and he could feel the heat rising from her skin. "Because if you sleep with me once, you'll sleep with me twice?"

Her cheeks turned a delicious shade of pink. "I can't believe I said that. Sometimes I speak before I think."

"I appreciated your directness." He reached out and tucked a loose tendril behind her ear. "What do you want, Julia? What did you come to New York for? I can get it for you."

She pulled her head away from his touch. "I don't want anything from you."

"Everyone wants something." *I want to fuck you, Julia. Again and again until I get you out of my head.* He pulled her to him and closed his mouth over hers. She met his mouth hungrily. He claimed her tongue with his own and reveled in her responsiveness. Where he led, she eagerly followed. Picking her up, he carried her over to his desk, pushing everything impatiently aside before sitting her on it so he could free his hands for more important things.

He told himself to go slowly, but the desire that burned in her blue eyes was his undoing. He needed to see her. To taste her. Without taking his eyes from hers, he tore the front of her shirt open, sending buttons flying. Her mouth dropped opened in an audible sigh and he was lost.

He pushed her knees farther apart and stepped between them. He leaned forward, ran his hand up her back beneath her now-open shirt, and arched her toward him. Her nipples were hard little nubs beneath her satin bra. Nubs he couldn't resist. He took one hungrily into his mouth, even through the material. Warming it with his tongue. Teasing it with his teeth.

She moaned and pressed herself upward and deeper into his mouth, and that was all the encouragement he needed. He ran a hand along the back of her bra and smiled against her skin when he found no clasp.

Whoever created front-release bras was a genius.

Gio eagerly unclasped the front of the bra and paused to appreciate the perfection that was Julia. She raised her head, her eyes glazed with passion, and he understood her need. His hand rubbed and lightly pinched one of her nipples while his mouth adored and feasted upon the other. Then he moved his mouth and paid her other breast equal attention.

She clung to his shoulders, then buried one hand in his hair. He ground his hard cock against her through their clothes. Desire surged within him. He couldn't get enough of her. Every taste of her pushed whatever control he had further and further away. He impatiently reached for the fastening of her pants.

"Knock, knock," a jovial male voice said from the doorway. "Well, will wonders never cease? I wouldn't have believed it if I hadn't seen it with my own eyes."

Raising his head reluctantly from Julia's neck, Gio turned, shielding her from his brother Luke's view. "What are you doing here?"

Smiling unabashedly, Luke leaned against the doorjamb. "Rena called me and said you were having a rough day, and I was ending a shift at the hospital anyway. She thought you might want to talk. It appears she was wrong."

"Get the hell out of here."

Still smiling, Luke wiggled his eyebrows and asked, "You're not going to introduce me?" Normally Luke was the most reasonable of his brothers, but presently his curiosity was outweighing his survival instincts.

"No," Gio said with finality.

"I heard you're coming to the wedding and bringing someone with you. Is this her?" His smile widened and his eyes twinkled with humor.

Gio aggressively rose to his full height. "You won't live to find out if you don't leave now," he said. Luke put up both hands in playful resignation and left, still smiling as he turned away.

Releasing a calming breath, Gio turned around and instantly felt like an ass. Julia was clutching her now buttonless top closed and sliding off his desk. The mood was broken. "Sorry about that," he said gruffly.

Her half smile set his heart thudding in his chest again. "It's okay."

"I should have locked the door. I don't normally..."

With an adorable blush, Julia said, "I don't do this either." She picked up her purse and started edging away from him. "I'm going home now."

"No," he said much more forcibly than he meant to.

She tucked her shirt into her pants, overlapping the front in a way that covered her. "Yes." She waved a shaking hand in the direction of his desk. "I'm not this person. I don't know what to do with how you make me feel. But I do know that I need time to think about this."

He reached for her, but she made it to the door before he could grab her.

When she opened her mouth to say something, he picked up his cell phone and said, "Todd, have a car brought around."

"I don't—" she started to say, but he cut her off.

"I'm taking you home."

As they walked down the hallway together, she sighed and said, "I'm not judging, but your whole family is a little pushy. You might want to try asking instead of issuing orders."

Her comment brought a smile back to his face. He placed his hand on her lower back and felt her tense when he replied, "Why ask when the outcome isn't in question?"

"Are you always this much of an arrogant ass?" she asked crossly.

With an ironic smile, he said, "No, normally, I'm much, much worse."

☙

Julia didn't know if he was joking or not, but she chuckled. "Don't make me laugh. It makes it harder to say no." She looked up at him and frowned. "And it is no. Just to be clear."

They rode down in the elevator and walked out of the building together in silence. The chauffer opened the door to a Bentley town car and she and Gio slid in. She told the driver her address and he pulled into traffic.

She snuck a peek at Gio. When he thought she wasn't looking there was an expression in his eyes that seemed almost sad. Was that the pain Maddy had mentioned? What had this man been through that kept him away from family who obviously loved him? She shouldn't ask. Shouldn't get involved. It would be easier to walk away if she didn't know.

And walk away is what she intended to do.

He wasn't looking for love; he was looking for a way into her pants. The problem was, every time she was near him she forgot why that was a bad idea. It didn't matter that they were both fully dressed and separated by a few inches. Her body tightened and warmed for his touch. If he took her into his arms right then, she doubted anything would stop them from finishing what they had started earlier. Not the fact that they were in public or that the driver would see them.

Why does this feel different than anything I've ever done?

I've dated a couple of men.

Men who made me laugh.

And sex with them was nice. It was a sweet expression of our feelings for each other.

But nothing like this. This is dangerous. I could lose myself if I'm not careful. She peered at him out of the corner of one eye and studied his strong profile. *But what a way to go.*

"I didn't realize you knew my cousin," he said, still looking straight ahead.

"I didn't, but she thinks I'm the reason you said yes to the wedding."

"You are," he said simply, and she swung around to search his face.

Julia swallowed hard. "I haven't changed my mind about not going."

He didn't answer. As they pulled up to her apartment building, he demanded, "You live here?"

Offended, Julia sat straight up. "It's clean. Relatively safe. And only one block from the subway."

He nodded toward what looked like a drug deal going down on the corner of the street.

She shrugged. "They're just kids. They've never bothered me."

He pinched the bridge of his nose. "You can't stay here."

She put her hands on her hips and turned in her seat. "Where I live is none of your business. This is what I can afford, and I don't appreciate you trying to make me feel badly about it."

"You're not staying here."

"Yes, I am."

He glared at her.

She glared back.

With a shake of his head, he said, "Gather your stuff. I'm checking you into a hotel."

The words sent unwanted shivers of pleasure down her back. *No. No. No. Down, libido.* She put her hand on the door handle. "Thank you for the ride home." She quickly opened the door and stepped out before he could stop her.

He was beside her in a heartbeat, blocking her escape. "Get back in the car."

"No."

He grabbed her arm. One of the youths across the street called out, "Hey, is he bothering you?"

She called back. "No, he's going." She met Gio's eyes angrily and said, "You are—going. Just because I work for you doesn't mean you have any right to tell me what I can do or where I can live. Let go of my arm."

Gio dropped her arm. "I don't understand you."

I don't understand me either, so we're even. "Goodnight, Mr. Andrade."

Julia turned and walked away, leaving him on the street watching her. Once she got inside, she didn't go to the window of her apartment. She didn't want to know if he was still there.

She wasn't sure she'd be able to stop herself from running back down and throwing herself in his arms.

This is for the best.

Whatever animal attraction we have for each other is the kind of chemistry that always leads to trouble.

Remember why you came to New York.

Stay focused.

She changed into her nightgown and made herself a microwave dinner.

Who wanted a date with a hot billionaire anyway?

Chapter Nine

RENA KNOCKED ON Gio's door, then walked into his office without waiting for his answer. "Do you have a minute?"

In the middle of a phone call, Gio raised one hand, told the governor courting him to invest in his state to send him some stats, and hung up the phone. He stood and stretched. Unable to sleep the night before, he'd come back to his office and worked through the night—something he was able to do since so many of his contacts were international. Although he was tired, it was a good tired. Work had always done that for him. When nothing else made sense, business did. He looked down at his watch. "Eight o'clock already? Get Atwater on the phone. I read over his proposal. It's promising, but some of his assumptions about our role in developing the area are way off. I'll give him access to our lobbyists, but I don't want our name linked publicly with his project. It's not going to be a popular one."

Rena closed the door behind her. "Before I do that... I want to apologize for last night. Luke called me after seeing you. I didn't mean to embarrass you."

"Forget it," he said gruffly.

Rena walked farther into his office. "We've known each other a long time, Gio. I feel like I grew up with you as a second brother. I know you hate when I get personal at work, but I'm worried about you. Did you actually reallocate one of your security team to watch Julia's apartment building?" She laid a hand flat on his desk, real concern evident in her expression. "What are you doing, Gio? This isn't like you."

Turning away from the concern in her eyes, Gio walked to look out the expansive office window. "I had to do something. The neighborhood she lives in isn't safe."

"Did she ask you for help?"

"Hell, no," Gio said, running his hand through his hair. "She told me the area was fine. I offered her an out, but she wanted to stay there. I don't understand her."

"That's because she's not like the women you usually date."

He rubbed his forehead in frustration. "Tell me about it."

"Did you really ask her to go to the island wedding with you?" Rena said with a smile in her voice.

"How do you—" He shook his head in resignation. "Don't tell me. I'd rather not know how you heard that. It doesn't matter. She said no."

"Which is fortunate for you, because you don't believe in workplace relationships."

"Exactly."

"Want my opinion?"

He groaned. "Not really, but I've never successfully convinced you to keep it to yourself."

"Go slow with this one. Take a walk with her. Share a coffee. Get to know her."

"What happened to, 'Stay the hell away from her? You're not ready for a nice woman'?"

"According to Luke, that horse has left the gate. Just be careful with her, Gio. You could really hurt her."

Looking out over the skyline, Gio listened to Rena's footsteps retreating across the office, then the door opening.

"And take a shower. You look like hell."

Gio closed his eyes for a moment and shook his head.

A walk?

It wasn't what he was craving to do with Julia, but nothing else had worked with her thus far. He was willing to try anything. The small taste he'd had of her had only heightened his desire for her. He couldn't look at his desk without imagining her there, half-dressed and ready for him. He could almost smell her soft perfume, hear the moan she made. He wanted to hear his name on her lips while she came for him.

He loosened his tie and threw it over the back of one of the chairs, then headed for the side door to his office. He did need a shower. A cold one.

C3

Julia had spent the day debating if she should return to Cogent Solutions or not. After walking out on a night she was scheduled, there was a good chance she was no longer employed. She finally decided that no matter how awkward it was, she would keep going until someone told her not to. *Landlords don't care that you almost slept with your boss the night before. They want their rent.*

And I'm not ready to go home yet.

She walked up to where Paul and Tom were sitting and asked, "Do you guys know if I'm scheduled for tonight?"

"As far as I know," Tom said as he pulled out a schedule sheet. "Yep. You're on the list. What happened last night? Mr. Andrade came down here asking for you. He didn't look happy."

Memories flooded back. Julia shook her head wordlessly at Tom. She didn't like to lie, but there was no part of yesterday that she was willing to repeat. *Thank God I didn't actually sleep with him. I'm already a mess.*

She turned to walk away and gasped when she saw Gio standing beside her.

"Let's take a walk," he said curtly.

Is this where he tells me that he can't believe I didn't realize I don't work here anymore? Let him say it. I've done nothing wrong. Okay, I've done a few things wrong, but all of that was just as much his fault as it was mine. It takes two. "I don't mind if they hear."

At least then I know we'll stay on safe topics.

He looked over at Paul and Tom, who were practically hanging over the security desk to hear what they were saying.

They instantly sat down and looked away. "We can't talk here. Come to my office."

She stepped back and shook her head. "I'm already late for my shift."

One corner of his mouth twitched as if he'd almost smiled. "I'm sure it will be fine."

Hitching her purse higher on her uniform-clad shoulder, Julia said, "I need this job. If you have a security-related concern, I'll be happy to discuss it with you—although I believe you will find Paul or Tom more knowledgeable. If I'm fired, you can tell me right here."

"You're not fired, but we do have something we need to discuss."

It would be so easy to give in. She fought to retain some control. "If it's a personal topic, I have a break at seven."

His jaw tightened. "Are you serious?"

She raised her chin. "Yes."

"Then I'll see you at seven." He turned and walked away.

Julia let out a long, shaky sigh.

Seven o'clock.

What does he want to talk to me about?

And how am I going to be able to wait until then to find out?

Chapter Ten

AT SEVEN O'CLOCK sharp, the phone on her desk rang. When she answered, Paul said from the other end of the line, "Mr. Andrade just exited the elevator. Do you want me to stall him?"

"No, Paul. It's good. I'll be right out."

With a quick look in a compact mirror, Julia hesitated. *If I freshen my lipstick now, it'll look like I did it for him. Like I'm expecting him to ask me out again.* She made a face in the mirror and chided herself.

It's more likely that he's looking for a way to dismiss me without this becoming a big deal. He's had time to think about it and he's as embarrassed as I am by what we did—or almost did.

She decided to apply a fresh coat of lipstick after all. *I'm going to need all the help I can get to survive hearing him list why sex with me is no longer a good idea.*

With one final fortifying breath, she opened the door and walked out into the foyer. *Mistakes are like ladder rungs to success. Embrace them. Learn from them.* She couldn't remember which article she'd found that quote in, but right then it didn't matter. She was embracing that quote along with her mistakes. Hugging the shit out of both them, really.

And forcing a brave smile to her face. "Mr. Andrade."

"Gio," he said smoothly and took her by the arm, guiding her out of the foyer and out the front door of the building. "Let's go outside," he said, his tone giving no hint to where this conversation was headed.

"Sure," Julia said slowly, keeping step beside him. Not that she had much of a choice. He wasn't letting go of her arm. *Oh, my God. Just tell me whatever it is you want to say.*

After about a block, his pace slowed and his hold on her relaxed. Without looking down at her, he said, "About last night..."

Trying to sound casual, she said, "I vote we forget it ever happened and move on."

He stopped and she nearly crashed into him. Even with people jostling around them on the sidewalk, the world seemed to disappear and nothing mattered but him and how she felt when she looked into his eyes. "Easier said than done."

Tell me about it. She bit her bottom lip and waited, her heart beating wildly in her chest.

"I've told you how I feel about office relationships."

Slam. Of course. Disappointment rose like bile in her throat. "Yes."

"The only solution is you quit. You're a distraction I don't need at work. I'll help you find another job. Not right away, of course. I'd like you to be free to travel with me. You'll have to move, though. Your living arrangements are completely unacceptable. I'll set you up in an apartment on the nice side of town. If you're worried about money, I can give you a generous allowance."

A slow burning anger started deep in Julia's stomach. Between gritted teeth she said, "Sounds like you put a lot of thought into this offer."

"I did," he said, so calmly that she wanted to kick him.

"And never once did it sound offensive to you? I can't believe I was upset because I thought you were going to say you didn't want to see me again." She threw her hair back over her shoulder. "You make me so angry I could strangle you." She poked a finger into his suit-covered shoulder. "And not in some funky, paid-mistress way. I mean actually hurt you."

He pulled her to him and the kiss they shared channeled her anger into a frenzied passion. Her hands flew to the back of his head and she ground against him, unable to deny the pull between them. His hands cupped her from behind, grinding her against his pulsing erection.

"Get a room," someone said behind them, but the taunt wasn't enough to pierce through their haze of sexual need. They stumbled backward against the side of a building, and Julia finally understood why people risked everything for this. There was something exquisitely, almost painfully, beautiful about giving in to a primal need and leaving the rest of the world behind.

His hand was sliding up her rib cage beneath her shirt when a camera flashed and someone said, "Got it."

He pulled back. "Shit." He reached for the photographer, but the young man was too fast and disappeared into the busy stream of people. His face tight with anger, and his eyes still storming with unfulfilled passion, he said, "This is exactly why we can't continue as we are..."

Julia's head was still spinning from the kiss. "I did not mean for that to happen." She covered her lips with one shaking hand.

"I did." He looked down at her intently and then, with his hand on the small of her back, guided her toward his office building. "Maybe now you'll stop pretending we don't want the same thing."

She looked up at him sadly. "I don't know what kind of women you're used to dating, but I don't want your money. I don't need you to pay for an apartment for me. And I'm offended that you think I would."

"Then tell me what you do want."

Julia looked away and then back at him. She had difficulty forming coherent thoughts when he was around her, but if he cared enough to ask, then she felt he should get an honest answer. "All the normal stuff. Ask me out. Send me roses. I'm partial to pink ones."

He didn't look happy with her answer, nor did he flat out reject the idea. They reentered Cogent Solutions together. He walked her to the door of her station, not seeming to care that all eyes were on them as he did. "I don't know what we're doing, but God help me, I can't stop myself when it comes to you." After one final, deep kiss that left Julia sagging against the wall, he walked away.

Julia was still standing there, watching him go, when she heard Paul say, "See. When a woman is that beautiful, no man is immune."

"Shut up, Paul," Tom said.

Still floating from the kiss, Julia wasn't bothered by the commentary. She returned to her station, sat down, and hoped no one decided to break into the building that night because her attention was definitely not on the monitors.

❦

Back in his office, Gio sat down at his desk and picked up his phone. Years of erasing stories in the media had given him the contacts necessary to ensure that photo wouldn't see print. It wasn't an easy feat in this day of the Internet, but people rarely published anything unless there was potential profit in it. The trick to getting a story killed was to make sure that remaining silent was more profitable for the source; or safer for their career.

He preferred to keep things positive, but he'd go to whatever lengths he needed when it came to protecting what was his.

And Julia fit that definition, regardless of how she might try to fight it.

She would be his.

Even though she fought him at every turn. He closed his eyes as he remembered how he hadn't cared who was around them on the street. He'd wanted her with such urgency that the photographer had done them a favor. A few more minutes and they might have started shedding clothing and given the press a story that even his contacts couldn't squash.

He groaned. After years of judging Nick for chasing everything in a skirt and mocking his lack of control, Gio was coming to the humbling conclusion that he had his own Achilles' heel—and her name was Julia.

And what did she want from him?

Flowers. He did a quick search on his phone for a flower shop, then placed an order that the florist repeated twice to make sure she'd heard correctly.

Would he like to include a message?

Oh, yes.

Chapter Eleven

THE LONG-STEMMED pink roses started arriving the next morning in an abundance that revealed Gio had no idea how small her apartment was. Once she'd packed them into her tiny kitchenette, the window sill, all of the floor space around her bed, and even put a few in the bathroom, she'd asked the delivery man to hand the rest of the vases out on the street below.

Yes, at night the neighborhood showed its underbelly, but during the day its sidewalks were filled with regular people who were thrilled by this unexpected gift: mothers walking their young children, couples who felt the flowers were a sign from fate, and some street vendors she'd never seen smile until the florist pointed up toward her open window and offered them a bouquet. After their initial suspicion passed, many of them had held up the flowers and waved to her in thanks.

The entire experience had put a lasting smile on Julia's face. She hadn't opened the envelope that had accompanied the flowers. She knew who they were from and she wanted to savor the moment. When the last bouquet was given away, she closed her window, waded through a forest of roses, and sat cross-legged in the middle of her bed.

She held the envelope to her chest but still didn't open it. *He's doing what I asked him to, but what do I have in common with a man like Gio? It would never work out. He wants sex. Hot. Glorious. Repeated sex. And he's willing to do anything to get me to agree.*

That's not love.

That's late-night porn.

Something he's already offered to pay me for. That's what being his mistress would be. A socially acceptable payment for sex.

Even these flowers. One thousand long-stemmed fuck-me-please flowers.

I didn't think he'd actually send them.

Or that I'd love the gesture as much as I do.

She picked one of the flowers out of a vase on the floor beside her bed and raised it to her nose, closing her eyes in pleasure as the scent filled her senses. The soft petals brushed against her bottom lip, reminding her how his mouth had fit so perfectly over hers. Her body didn't care about the poor timing of this temptation; it flooded with heat at the memory of being pushed up against the side of a New York building with a passion that had robbed both of them of their inhibitions.

She opened her eyes and studied the envelope again.

Does it include an invitation to somewhere?

It doesn't matter.

The flowers don't actually change anything.

I'd be better off spending the day in the Diamond District trying to make a connection than being pulled, albeit willingly, into something I know is wrong for me.

Call him at work.

Thank him and politely refuse to take this further.

Don't read the card.

Once you open that door, you won't be able to close it.

You won't be strong enough to say no.

She lay back on the bed and covered her eyes with the paper.

Her phone began to vibrate on the nightstand beside her bed. She rolled onto her stomach. Unknown number. She held her breath and answered it. "Hello?"

"Good morning, Julia," Gio said, his voice warm and intimate.

She sat straight up in her bed and dropped the card. "Mr. Andrade."

"We're way beyond using last names and you know that."

Protectively pulling down her nightgown to cover her knees, Julia said huskily, "About that. Thank you for the flowers, but—"

"Did I wake you?"

"No, the delivery did that," she said, then felt bad that she sounded ungrateful. This wasn't going as she'd planned.

"So, you're not on your bed? I have an image in my head of you there, surrounded by those roses."

The heat from a blush spread up Julia's chest and warmed her cheeks. She knew she shouldn't, but she couldn't help herself. She said, "I am on my bed." Then she hastily added, "But only because it doubles as my couch."

He groaned. "I refuse to sink low enough to ask you what you're wearing, but if you want to describe it I won't stop you."

There was something irresistibly tempting about doing just that. Was it the knowledge that in that moment she had the same power over him that he had over her? The sense that he was fighting this as much as she was?

It proved too heady to resist. "I'm still in my nightgown."

He let out a long breath. "If I were there it wouldn't be on you for long. Take it off, Julia. For me."

Her first response was to laugh and refuse, but his softly spoken order echoed through her and her body started humming with need for him. As she gave into it, it became impossible to deny him anything. She slid the nightgown over her head and lay back, fully naked on her bed. "It's off," she whispered.

The pained sound he made had her dripping wet and closing her eyes, imagining him there with her.

"Lick your thumb. Lick it, then circle one of your nipples. Imagine my tongue there. I wouldn't be able to keep my mouth off you. What would you want me to do to them?"

What would have felt ridiculous with anyone else was somehow right with Gio. She did as he asked, gasped as the cold air tightened and puckered her nipple with pleasure. She imagined that her hand was his mouth. Her fingers were his teeth. She pinched herself lightly and moaned. "I'd want you to use your teeth gently. Like you did in your office. Tugging. Teasing. Oh, God, this is crazy."

"You're killing me, but don't stop, Julia. I'm here with you. Right here. What would you want me to do? What do you like?"

She ran her hand up her neck and pushed her hair aside. "I love the feel of your hot breath on my neck, the feel of your lips claiming where I'm vulnerable."

"I'll remember that. I'll start there and kiss my way down, slowly. I'll kiss the curve of your waist, the silk of your thighs. I'll want to dive into you, but I'll make you wait until you're writhing and begging for me to taste you."

That would not take long, Julia almost said aloud.

"Are you wet for me, Julia?"

"Yes," she said, giving herself to him fully in the safety of the situation. Her hand sought her own juices and she began to rub herself. "Oh, God, I am so wet."

"Do you have a vibrator?" he asked and her hand froze.

I can't tell him.

She did have one, but it was her guilty secret. One that she hadn't even shared with her ex-boyfriend, even after sleeping with him.

"You do, don't you? Are you shy about it? Sex is a natural part of life, Julia. There is nothing shameful about knowing how to please yourself. In fact, I want you more now. I want to watch you make yourself come. I want to lie next to you, caressing you as you bring yourself to climax. But for now, let me hear it. Take yourself to where we both want to go."

Frantically, Julia flung out a hand and opened the drawer on the nightstand beside her bed. Her hand closed on the six-inch toy she'd never admitted to owning. With a quick twist she turned it on and brought it to her eager clit.

"That's it, Julia. Oh, God, you are so hot. Dip it inside of you. Deep inside. That will be me. Soon."

She drove the toy deep inside her with one thrust and called out, "Gio."

"Oh, yes. Say my name. I want to be on your lips. I want to be in your head. When you come, I want my name to be what you call out."

With increasing speed, Julia plunged the vibrator inside of her and pulled it out, sliding it against her throbbing nub as she did. In and out. Faster and faster, until she dropped the phone next to her, grabbed the comforter next to her with one grasping hand, and cried out Gio's name as she surrendered to her shuddering, glorious orgasm.

Neither of them spoke. As Julia came back down to earth, she grew self-conscious, as if he could see her. She pulled the comforter over her head quickly and stashed her vibrator back in the drawer.

She groaned. *What am I doing?*

"Julia." He said her name like it was a command.

She's not here.

She buried her face in a pillow for a moment. *No wonder he thinks he can offer me money for sex. What is wrong with me?*

"Pick up the phone or I'm coming over," he said in a determined voice, and Julia knew he meant it.

With her face still buried in the pillow, she held her cell phone to her ear. "I am so embarrassed. I may never leave my apartment again."

"You? I'm sitting at my desk with a hard-on the likes of which I haven't seen since puberty. If I had known this was how I would start my day, I would have locked the door and joined you. I almost did, but lately someone would have walked in, and everyone is pretty sure I've lost my mind already. Because of you I'm going to be late for my meeting. I want to appear excited about the project, but not this excited."

Julia chuckled reluctantly, but she wasn't coming out of hiding yet. "I spent the morning rehearsing how to tell you that I'm not interested in whatever you wrote on the card."

"You didn't open it?"

"No, I was trying to remain strong."

This time he chuckled, and she threw the pillow across the room as if he were there to get hit by it. "It's not funny. I don't do stuff like this. I'm really a pretty boring person once you get to know me. You need a woman who... someone who..."

"Stop talking, Julia, and open the card."

She sat up and did as he asked. Well, asked was putting it nicely. He was back to using the authoritative tone that made her want to defiantly stick her tongue out at him.

But not more than she wanted to know what he'd written. She tore the envelope open.

"Pick any dress you want and wear it for me tonight. We have a reservation at Le Loire at eight."

Without thinking, she said, "I'm working tonight."

"I already covered your shift."

"You did what? Without even asking me?"

"The outcome was never in question."

"It most certainly was... I mean... is."

"I'll pick you up at seven thirty."

"I haven't said yes."

"If you're not dressed for dinner I'll assume you want to spend the evening alone with me... in your bed."

"What if I'm not here?" she asked, desperately trying to regain control of the situation.

"I'll find you. You can't run from this, Julia, any more than I can. Go to the address on the card and get yourself something nice. On me. Something you know I'll enjoy taking off you as much as you'll enjoy wearing." He hung up.

Julia held up the business card of a small, elite boutique on the Upper East Side.

I would tell myself that I'm not going dress shopping today, but I am really bad at saying no to this man.

ଔ

Two hours later, Julia was craning her neck to see how the back of the sleeveless floor-length black gown she was modeling shimmered in the changing-room mirror. She would have gone out into the main area, but she didn't want to talk to the clerk. Talking about the dress meant she was actually doing this. She was letting a rich man buy her a dress, take her out, and then most likely take her home.

She wasn't ready to defend that choice yet.

But she had to admit, the dress fit her perfectly.

If she was the kind of girl who did something this spontaneous, this was definitely how she'd dress to do it.

The light caught the gemstones in her gold necklace and brought its floral design to life. It wasn't an overly expensive piece, but she'd used real metals to make it. She'd worn it to help her remember what was really important. Family. Duty. Finding a buyer and going home to save her father's company.

She spun in front of the mirror.

This was nothing more than a distraction from that.

But what a wonderfully magical distraction it was.

She and her parents had always lived a modest life. Even when business had been good, her parents hadn't been the type to care about material things. She'd grown up in a beach town, spending most of her free time in the summers on the beach in a bikini and shorts, or serving ice cream to tourists. During cooler weather, she'd holed up in her jewelry workshop, which her father had created for her at his furniture factory. It didn't matter to him that it didn't make sense to do it. He'd done it for her. Just like he'd added a jewelry section to his showroom floor. Not because it was good for business, but because he thought she was talented and her work deserved to be displayed.

Oh, Dad.

Is this how you felt when you met Mom? Or am I making the biggest mistake of my life?

I know I should walk away from this situation, but I can't.

I want to see him again.

The clerk's voice rose and broke into her thoughts. "Mrs. Rockport. I didn't know you were coming in today. I'd close the boutique for you now, but I have a woman in the back trying on some dresses."

An older woman's voice answered curtly, "As long as she's not some simpering, preening fool I'm sure I'll be able to overlook her presence."

"Yes, Mrs. Rockport. Yvonne isn't here today. Are you looking for something off the rack?"

"If she were here I would already have a glass of champagne in my hand. Not that she carries the good stuff, but it's the courtesy that matters." After a brief pause, the older woman said, "What are you waiting for? Go get one."

Crotchety old bitch.

Julia admonished herself for the thought. *Money doesn't make people happy. She's probably miserable and lonely. Why else would she come to the shop alone when someone like her could have whatever she wanted delivered?*

Turning her attention back to the mirror, Julia held her hair up and studied it from the side. *No, I'll feel like I'm going to prom. Simple is better.* She sternly looked at herself in the mirror again. *Not that I'm going.* She let her hair drop, then brought her hands up to undo the zipper, but it was caught.

Oh, great.

She tried again without success.

Maybe I can get it over my head without unzipping it.

The material fit her too snuggly.

In resignation she opened the dressing-room door and stepped out. Giving in to an inner impish impulse, she walked over to the older woman, who had maintained her health into what looked like her late seventies. She stopped in front of her, turned, and spoke over her shoulder to her. "Do you mind unzipping me?"

The woman's mouth dropped open. "Excuse me?"

Kill them with kindness. That was her father's motto—and honestly, sometimes it was fun to do. She pretended not to understand that the older woman found the request distasteful. "The zipper is stuck. Could you give it a little pull?"

"Do I look like I work here?" the woman asked in a tone a queen might use in the presence of one of her filthiest subjects.

Then a bit of her no-nonsense mother came out. Turning around to face the woman, Julia said bluntly, "No. I've found the people who work here to be quite pleasant."

"Unbelievable. They will let anyone shop here now, won't they? I've never, in all of my life, met anyone so without class."

With a sweet smile, Julia said, "I have. I heard you talking to the clerk. You know what? I don't care how much money you have, you shouldn't treat people that way. She probably makes just over minimum wage plus commission, so she has to kiss your ass, but I don't. You weren't nice to her, but you should have been. I feel sorry for you if you can't see that."

A slow red spread up the woman's face. She opened her mouth, then closed it with a snap.

The clerk returned and, with a shaking hand, handed a glass to the older woman, who accepted it and said, "Thank you." A show of manners that seemed to surprise the clerk. Then she said, "You may want to help this young lady out of her dress. She's trapped."

The clerk said in a rush, "It'll only take a moment."

With an expression Julia couldn't decipher, the older woman said, "Take your time."

Julia returned to the dressing room, followed by the young clerk. Once inside, the woman made quick work of untangling the material that had wedged inside the zipper. Then she met Julia's eyes in the mirror and said, "I heard what you said to her. You have no idea how many times I've wanted to tell her off, but I need this job."

"My father always says that people treat others the way they feel on the inside. She can't be a happy woman."

From across the floor, Mrs. Rockport said, "Until just now I had no idea that the dressing rooms were not soundproof."

Julia and the clerk hunched over in a shared guilty laugh they fought to contain.

The clerk said, in a much softer tone than she'd used before, "She heard us. I am so fired."

If there was one thing working in her father's showroom had taught Julia, it was how to calm a disgruntled customer. "I'll fix this," she whispered.

Changing hastily back into her jeans and blouse, Julia squared her shoulders and went to face the woman, hoping to smooth some ruffled feathers. The clerk would likely spend the rest of the day hiding in the changing room if it didn't work. She walked directly over to the woman and said, "Don't be upset with the clerk. This was my fault. My mouth gets ahead of my brain sometimes. That was unforgivably rude of me. I apologize."

Settling somewhat, Mrs. Rockport said, "Everyone has an off day. I, myself, woke up in a foul mood."

Julia hid her grin but couldn't hold her tongue. "It didn't show at all."

The woman narrowed her eyes, then let out a bark of a laugh. "You have spunk, don't you? I was like you when I was younger. Outspoken long before it was fashionable to be so."

Julia's face split in a genuine smile. "I can see you as a firecracker."

"Oh, I was. My father feared I'd never settle down." She looked wistful as old memories brought a small smile to her face, but the moment was short-lived. "I did, of course. Everyone does." She sat down as if suddenly tired, then said, "So, tell me about the man you're buying that dress for."

"I'm not buying it," Julia said in a rush. "I could never afford something like that."

The woman looked her over shrewdly. "So, he's buying it for you?"

"Maybe," Julia said and plopped down on the seat next to the woman who a moment ago had been an adversary. "I shouldn't let him. Really, if I had any sense, I wouldn't even see him again." Without waiting for a response from the older woman, Julia said, "He's rich and used to getting what he wants. I come from a working-class family. I don't care which fork is the right one to use at dinner, and he was probably born knowing that sort of thing. All we really have in common is—" Julia stopped and blushed. "I'm sorry, I don't know why I'm sharing this with you."

Mrs. Rockport quietly studied her for a moment, then said, "I married my first husband against my father's wishes. He didn't come from money. In fact, when I met him he didn't even have a job. But he had dreams and a smile that could make a foolish decision seem like the only one that made sense."

Julia turned in her seat. "What happened?"

"We had one magical year, then the Korean War started and he signed up to go. His friends were going and, even though my father would have helped him dodge the draft, he wanted to serve his country." Her face twisted a bit. "He never came home."

Julia put her hand on the woman's and wiped a tear away with her other. "I'm so sorry to hear that."

Mrs. Rockport patted her hand and recomposed herself. "It was a long time ago. I married again. He was a good man who loved me very much. He died, too, a few years ago." She took a deep breath. "You can make all the plans you want, but life has a way of turning out however the hell it wants to, no matter what you do. And in the end, all you have are memories."

Uncharacteristically, Julia was speechless.

The older woman laced her fingers in thought. "Let your man buy you that dress. Give yourself something to smile about when you're my age."

Julia blushed and instinctively touched her necklace. Would everything work out the way it was supposed to, even if she let herself look away long enough to build those memories?

"That's a beautiful piece you're wearing," Mrs. Rockport said.

Julia smiled. "I designed it. The gems aren't real. When I have my own business one day it will have real stones, but for now that's just a dream."

"May I?"

Julia nodded and the woman touched it lightly.

"It looks like something my sister would have worn. She loved flowers and diamonds."

Following an impulse, Julia took the necklace off and put it in the woman's hand. "I'd like you to have it."

Mrs. Rockport tried to hand it back. "I couldn't possibly."

Julia pressed it into her hand and said, "More than anything else, I am an artist. And for me there is no greater pleasure than knowing something I've created has touched someone's heart. If it reminds you of your sister, you should have it. I can make another."

Clearing her throat, the woman fingered the necklace gently, then nodded. "I would pay you, of course."

Julia shook her head. "I wouldn't take it."

"You're an awful businesswoman," the woman chided gently.

"Maybe," Julia said with a rueful smile.

They sat there quietly for a moment, then Mrs. Rockport asked, "So, are you getting the dress?"

Julia nodded shyly and blushed again.

"Claudia," the older woman called out to the clerk. "I'm feeling spontaneous today. Please have one of each dress here wrapped and sent to a local charity. Tell Yvonne I want a list of where they went. But make sure you get credit for the sale. Put it on my account."

After double-checking she'd heard right, the clerk rushed off to ring up the sale.

"What's your name?" Mrs. Rockport asked.

"Julia. Julia Bennett."

The woman stood and held out her hand. "It was a pleasure to meet you, Miss Bennett. I hope our paths cross again."

Julia couldn't imagine how they would, but she shook the woman's hand warmly and said she hoped the same.

Alone in the boutique again, she asked the clerk to box up the dress and held it tightly the entire taxi ride home.

Am I about to create memories I'll treasure for a lifetime?

Or make a mistake that will haunt me?

And are women nearing eighty a reliable source for sexual advice?

Chapter Twelve

GIO WATCHED JULIA pour over the menu in a way none of the many women he'd brought here ever had. Food was not why people came to Le Loire, the theater district's highly exclusive restaurant. They came because reservations were booked more than a year out and merely getting a table meant that you had arrived in some way at the top of New York's social stratosphere. They came to see and be seen.

A quick look around the dining area revealed a collection of New York's wealthiest and visiting famous. Gio wasn't impressed by either, but he knew most women were.

Dressed as she was, Julia blended perfectly with the crowd. He'd caught more than one of his peers eyeing her appreciatively. She wasn't the first beautiful woman he'd escorted in public. Normally he didn't care one way or another what others thought of his date, but when he caught one blatant male admirer staring at Julia's profile from a few tables away, he'd half risen out of his chair without thinking.

To what? Brawl?

The man had met his eyes, read his intent, and hastily looked away. Gio had let out a long breath and settled back into his seat, surprised by how possessive he already felt about the woman sitting across from him.

"Have you had the seafood here?" she asked, drawing him back from his thoughts.

"I'm sorry?"

"The plateau de fruits de mer. I love seafood, but I had this dish once at an expensive restaurant in Rhode Island and it was served with a tiny octopus and whole prawns. Some had eyes. I can't eat anything that still has eyes."

"I normally have the Kobe steak," he said, somewhat bemused by her level of animation. He'd never seen a woman order anything but a salad—dressing on the side, all possible calories or carbs banished from their meal. "Chef Cazon is excellent. I'm sure you'll be pleased with whatever you order."

"You can't come to a place like this and have steak," she said with a laugh. "How about this? I'll order for you and you order for me."

"Why?" he asked slowly.

She seemed as confused by his reluctance as he was by her suggestion. "Because it'll be fun?"

His idea of fun had more to do with what they would do after dinner, but he decided to humor her. He opened his menu. "What do you like?"

She put down the menu. "I'm not going to tell you. You have to try to figure it out."

"I don't play games," he said, more out of habit than from a real desire to end the exchange. He did want to know what she liked, and he intended to spend the rest of night exploring just that. He reached for a glass of water, seeking a calm that he'd more easily achieve by pouring the cool drink on his bulging crotch than by drinking it. *Slow down. No need to rush.*

She cocked her head to one side and said, "Maybe you should. Then you'd look less like you're constipated all the time."

He choked on the water, swallowed it the wrong way, and choked more.

She was up, out of her seat, and patting his back forcibly. "Are you okay?"

He stood, cleared his throat one final time, looked into her anxious eyes, and let out a laugh that echoed through the suddenly silent restaurant. He took one of her hands in his and said, "Sit down, Julia. I'm fine."

She looked around, realized that all eyes were on them, and returned to her seat in a rush—a beautiful pink flush on her cheeks. She picked up the menu again, this time hiding behind it. "I shouldn't have said that. Why don't I think before I speak?"

Gio reached across the table and took one of her hands in his. "You are refreshingly honest." The smile she gave him as a reward for his comment stole his breath away. Still, he couldn't resist teasing her a bit. "Constipated, huh?"

She blushed again. "Not literally. Emotionally. Like there is so much you want to say but you won't let yourself."

He dropped her hand as the words cut too close to home.

The sommelier came by and asked if Gio would be ordering his usual, or if he would like to see a wine menu. Gio said, "The usual." Then looked across at Julia. "Unless you have a preference."

"I don't drink."

"Not even one glass?" he asked.

"No one in my family drinks much." A warm smile spread across her face. "My father always said he'd rather get lost in Renoir than old grapes."

"That's an unusual viewpoint," Gio said, gesturing to the sommelier that they had finished their order.

"My father's a unique man, and perfect for my mother. They are the most amazing people in the most surprising ways. My father was a starving artist until he met my mother. He was everything her family didn't want for her. He came from a tough background. He had no money to speak of. But he loved her. She told me she knew from the first moment they met that he was the one for her. Just like that. They met. Wham—it hit both of them, and they were never apart after that. She helped him make a business out of his love of art. That's what people do when it's right. They bring out the best in each other. I know how lucky I am to have such great parents. And that's why I'm here."

The more she spoke, the more uncomfortable Gio felt. In some ways Rena was right. Julia sounded dangerously naive and innocent. Modern women didn't believe in love at first sight. They were practical—as jaded as he was. Rena was wrong, though, in thinking that getting to know Julia better would lessen how important their differences were.

He wanted to ask her what she'd meant by her parents being the reason she was here, but the waiter arrived and asked for their order. Instead of giving hers, Julia surprised both of them by asking, "Is it possible to speak with the chef?"

The waiter looked from her to Gio. Gio nodded and the waiter headed toward the kitchen.

"I'm sure the waiter would know which items do or do not have eyes," he said softly.

Julia smiled into his eyes but for once did not share her thoughts. The chef was at the table almost instantly.

"Mr. Andrade. It is a pleasure to have you join us again. What can I do for you?"

Gio sat back and gestured indulgently toward Julia. "Eli, it was Miss Bennett who had a question for you."

Julia enthusiastically put out her hand to the chef, who shook it politely.

"A pleasure, Miss Bennett."

"I heard a rumor that my dining partner tends to eat the same thing every time he comes here. I saw that you had a few items that were traditional dishes. Are those family recipes?"

A huge, pleased smile spread across his face. "Yes, they are. My mother visits a few times a year and insists that they remain on the menu."

"She must be so proud when she comes here. Which dish is her favorite?"

"She says the boeuf bourguignon reminds her of home. It's a simple beef stew in red wine with bacon, mushrooms, and onions."

"That sounds like the perfect comfort food. Does making it remind you of your childhood?"

"Yes," he said in surprise. "It would be my honor to make it for you."

Julia nodded and an impish smile stretched across her lips. "You seem to know Mr. Andrade. What would you pick for him?"

"I would not presume to know his taste."

"Humor her," Gio ordered softly. For a reason he couldn't pin down, it was important to him that Julia wasn't disappointed in this game.

With a shrug, the chef said, "Before tonight I would have said that his palate had become dull from his predictable diet. However, it looks like he's ready for a change, so I would suggest the sautéed langoustine with a summer truffle and chanterelle in a sweet sauce. I've added a few enhancing spices. It is mild and pleasing at first, but has a bite that is unforgettable."

"A bite?" Julia asked, missing the undercurrent of the conversation. "That sounds either delicious or dangerous."

Exactly what I was thinking myself. Gio nodded to the chef to approve the choice. Would a night of sex with Julia lessen the hunger within him or increase it?

He didn't know, but he was driven to find out.

The chef turned to Julia, raised her hand, and kissed it. "It was a real pleasure meeting you, Miss Bennett. I hope to see you again."

Julia blushed, and Gio was glad the chef retreated back to the kitchen before he made Gio say something that revealed how possessive he was becoming toward Julia.

಴

Julia watched the chef disappear into the kitchen, then groaned when she glanced back at Gio and caught him frowning at her. *I can't believe I told him he looked constipated. Who does that? Only me and my big nervous mouth.*

Then I practically strong-armed him into ordering a meal he'll probably hate.

On the up side, I won't have to worry if he'll ever ask me out again since he'll probably find an excuse to end this date early.

How many times had her ex-boyfriend told her to stop talking about her parents? "No one is interested," he'd said more than once. Julia knew it was more the norm for people to gripe about how they were raised, but she didn't have any horrific childhood stories to share. Before her mother had gotten sick, she couldn't remember a time when she hadn't been as happy to be around her parents as she was to be with her friends.

They're good people. I won't pretend to hate them just to sound cool.

Not that I have any chance of appearing sophisticated now that I led off with a reference to bowel blockage.

No wonder he's giving me that look.

At which point of a failed evening do you toss up the white surrender flag and call it as it is?

"You were telling me about how your parents were the reason you came to New York," Gio surprised her by saying.

He's just being polite. "It's a long story."

He held her eyes and took her hand. "I don't ask a question unless I'm interested in the answer."

"Are you sure?"

His grip on her hand tightened. "The one promise I will make you is that I won't lie to you, Julia. I've seen how destructive lies can be and I have no patience for them. You may not always like what I say, but it'll be the truth." He let out a long breath. "Now, tell me how being raised by these paragons of parents led you to a night-security job at my company."

The story spilled out of her, broken only momentarily by the arrival of their food. She told him about her mother's diagnosis of Alzheimer's a few years back and how the disease had progressively worsened. She described how their lives had changed as the woman who had always led the family could no longer remember if she had turned the stove on to heat water for her tea. "My father became her full-time caretaker, and that meant neither of them were able to maintain the business. I ran the actual store, but my father was supposed to be paying the taxes and the vendors. He fell behind and didn't tell me because he didn't want me to worry. By the time I found out, he was also behind on the mortgage. The bank threatened to auction off the land the factory and store are on. There are developers who are interested in that land. We have sixty days to come up with two hundred thousand dollars or the bank claims the property."

"That's not a lot of money. Surely the bank—"

"To you, that's not a lot of money. To people like me, it's a huge amount, and more than any bank would ever lend us."

He studied her quietly, then said, "I could loan you the money."

"If I sleep with you?" she countered, pulling her hand free of his.

"The loan would have nothing to do with what happens between us."

She shook her head in disbelief. "You said you wouldn't lie to me."

His face tightened and a slight flush spread up his cheeks. "Fine. I want you in my bed. Tonight. All night. And tomorrow night. I have a feeling that when I get you into my bed, you're going to be an addiction that takes me awhile to break. I don't want you working at my company. I don't want you living where you are. If that costs me the amount you need to help your father—so be it. I'll give you double if it gets me what I want."

Well, you ask for honesty—you get honesty.

Ouch.

"Do you pay all of your dates, or am I just the lucky one?"

"Most women are happy with jewelry and being seen in public with me, but I don't mind that you're more expensive. I told you, Julia. Tell me what you want and I'll make it happen."

Julia looked around the restaurant with new eyes. "And is this one of the places that you take those women?"

He didn't answer.

"Of course it is. You didn't take me here because this place is special to you. You brought me here because you bring everyone here. I should have known." She stood up and threw her napkin on her uneaten food. "Apologize to Chef Cazon for me. I just lost my appetite."

He stood and blocked her way. "Sit down, Julia."

"No," she said, and this time she didn't care who was watching. "You don't get it. I'm not for sale. If you really do want to be with me you're going to have to wake up and do a whole hell of a lot better than this." With that, she pushed past him and rushed out of the restaurant.

C

Gio almost followed her, but stopped when he saw she'd left her purse beside her chair. She wouldn't get far without it.

He took several large bills out of his wallet and threw them in the middle of the table, then bent to retrieve her purse. The waiter rushed over. "You're leaving, Mr. Andrade? Was there something wrong with the food?"

No, there is something wrong with me.

"The evening has merely taken an unexpected turn. Please make my apologies to the chef."

With that, he walked out of the restaurant with Julia's purse in his hand, not caring that the gossip rags would be abuzz with the story the next day. Right then, all he cared about was finding Julia.

They met on the street. She was headed back toward the restaurant. She walked up to him, gloriously decked out in her tight black dress and high heels. Her blue eyes were shooting daggers at him, and she'd never looked more beautiful to him. She stopped right in front of him and wordlessly held out her hand for her purse.

He didn't move to give it to her. Instead, he motioned for his driver to pull the town car around. "I chose the restaurant poorly."

Julia stubbornly folded her arms in front of her. "Yes, you did."

"I've never met anyone like you before, Julia. If you're confused, know that I share the feeling."

Relaxing somewhat, Julia looked away and then back at him, emotions darkening her eyes. "Money doesn't give you the right to treat people the way you do."

"It was not my intention to offend you." He handed her the purse.

She took it and hugged it to her stomach. "My mother didn't marry a man because she wanted something from him. She fell in love with my father and they built something together. You asked me why I came to New York and I started to tell you. But it's not only the money I'm looking for. I've spent my life very comfortably, being like my father. Joyfully lost in my art. No real responsibilities or worries. I see now how much my mother sheltered us."

Gio's heart started thudding painfully in his chest when Julia's eyes misted with tears. He was a man who took action, but in that moment he didn't know what to do.

"My mother is the strongest woman I know. I have to have that strength somewhere in me. I have to. If I can find it—I know I'll figure the rest out. Maybe I'll sell my jewelry to a chain, or I'll meet someone who is looking for a houseful of my dad's furniture. I don't know. But I do know what you're offering me is not what I'm looking for. I live where I can afford it. I work a job that allows me to network during the day, and hopefully I'll make connections that will lead to a solution. Not the solution you offered—but one I can live with." She looked down at the gown she was wearing. "I knew I had made a mistake when I left the store with this dress. I shouldn't have come here. This whole night was my fault. I'm sorry if I gave you the wrong impression."

Jaw tight, Gio said, "I don't believe in love. Not the selfless kind you're describing." He reached forward and with his thumb brushed away the tear that ran down her cheek. "Don't cry, Julia."

She couldn't help it. When it came to Gio, her emotions were raw and exposed.

"I've been selfish," he said. "I keep trying to make you into someone who'll fit into my life. I wish I had more to offer you, but I don't. I'm not looking for marriage. I don't want children. I've become so obsessed with getting into your bed that I told myself it doesn't matter. But it does matter—to you."

She smiled sadly. "I'm sorry."

He cupped her face in his hand, rubbing his thumb lightly over her lips. "It's not going to be easy knowing that you're downstairs."

She covered his hand with hers, then moved away from him. "It's not easy to say no."

"Get in the car," he said briskly.

"I meant what I said," she said urgently.

"My driver will take you home. I'm going to walk. I could use the fresh air."

She studied his expression intently, then nodded and stepped into the door the driver held open for her.

In the quickly cooling New York night, Gio walked the ten blocks back to his office building. He needed to clear his head with work.

Chapter Thirteen

A FEW DAYS later, Gio was at his desk reading over proposals on a possible new shale find in South America. The local governments were still discussing the feasibility of reaching it. The time was right to pick a horse in that race and invest. He would have preferred to finish one project before investing in another, but opportunities didn't wait until the timing was convenient. They arrived like a flash of lightning and left just as quickly.

He'd grown his family's company by knowing where these strikes would happen and being ready to harness their power when they did. Often, he was in and out of an area before his competition knew a door had opened.

He was decisive because hesitations cost money.

A knock on the door was instantly followed by its swinging open without waiting for his response. *This ends now.* Gio stood and roared his displeasure. "I said I was not to be disturbed."

"No wonder Rena called me. You look like shit." Rena's older brother, Kane, one of Gio's closest friends, walked in, completely unfettered by the greeting he'd received.

"Thanks. Don't you have a job for her at your company yet?" Still not smiling, he crossed the room to shake his friend's hand.

Although Kane now wore expensive suits and styled his hair conservatively, Gio would forever see his friend as he'd looked in college: unruly hair, defiantly spiked in front long before that was the fashion. Kane came from first-generation money, which brought its own challenges. Such children often struggled with addictions and excess. Luckily Kane and Rena's parents had instilled a good work ethic in both of them. "She's happy here," Kane said after shaking his hand. He gave his friend a long once-over. "When you're not yelling at her. She says you're having a rough week."

"She needs to learn to mind her own business."

"Yeah, good luck with that." Kane walked in and sat in Gio's chair, leaning back far enough that Gio was convinced the former quarterback would break it.

"Make yourself comfortable," Gio said in a harsh tone. Kane smiled. They were close like brothers, and apparently that relationship had given Kane immunity to a tone that would have intimidated other men.

"I also spoke to Luke. He said he's worried about you. Rena is worried about you. After the article I read in the paper the other day, I'll admit I'm a little concerned myself. The photo of you at Le Loire with that woman in a black dress preparing to give you the Heimlich maneuver was classic, but I think I preferred the one with you chasing her out the door with her purse."

Rubbing his tired eyes with both hands, Gio groaned. "I completely forgot to call anyone about those. Shit."

Sounding much too amused, Kane said, "The Internet is on fire with an article about it. 'Billionaire Bachelor With a Sensitive Side.' Rena said they have photos of you outside the restaurant caressing her face and looking longingly into her eyes. You've got it pretty bad for this one. Who is she?"

Gio turned away from his friend and looked out the window in frustration. "No one important."

Kane left the chair, and his tone turned serious. "I get it. You haven't been yourself since you came back from that engagement party with your uncles. If you're using this woman to cheer yourself up, fine. I just want to make sure she's not a symptom of something else going on that you're not sharing with anyone."

"If I had anything I wanted to talk to you about, I have your number."

"You say that, but looking at you, I don't believe it."

"Kane, I'll say this as kindly as I can. Go get a testosterone shot. You spend way too much time with your sister. You're beginning to sound like her."

"Sometimes she's right. Rena says this mystery woman works here. That's not your style."

If the conversation had been with anyone but Kane, it would have ended right now. Kane had been a good friend to him for too many years to take out his frustration on him. He closed his eyes for a moment, finding the calm he sought by shutting down inside. He opened his eyes, once again in control, and forced a smile. "I'm fine."

The joke removed the tension between them, but Kane still looked concerned. "I don't believe you. Are you going to tell me, or do I have to come back later and get you drunk? Midday tequila shots are no longer my style, but you look like you could use a few."

There wasn't a doubt in Gio's mind that Kane would return if he wasn't satisfied with how the conversation went, so Gio ground out, "What do you know, Kane?"

"Are you okay?"

Running his hand through his hair, Gio admitted the truth. "No."

"What's wrong?"

"I'm not sleeping. I'm not eating. I can't concentrate. There's something wrong with me."

"Maybe you're in love."

"Don't be a fucking idiot. I'm serious. I could have a brain tumor."

"I'll have to ask Luke, but I've never heard of a tumor causing a man to chase after a woman while clutching her purse. It is an illness, though. And, I hear, a degenerative one. Next you'll be buying her tampons."

Gio pinched the bridge of his nose in irritation. "I'm trying remember why we're friends, but right now it's difficult."

"Are you even dating this woman?"

"No."

"Screwing her?"

"No. I told you. She's nothing to me."

Shaking his head with humor, Kane said, "I wish I could help you, Gio, but you're already too far gone. What are you going to do?"

"Nothing. I considered her an option for something more, but it wasn't worth the trouble. You know how I feel about anything serious."

"You're such a pussy," Kane said.

"Excuse me?" Gio roared.

"You heard me. Rena says this is the type of woman a man marries. She said you're shaking in your shoes at the idea, and I think she's right. If you like this woman, date her. Don't hide in your office pretending that facial hair looks good on you."

"It's not that easy," Gio growled. Even the thought of Julia brought a swell of emotion to the surface—one that he fought to control. "I don't like who I am around her. I'm jealous. I'm impulsive. I say stupid shit."

Kane smiled sympathetically. "It eventually happens to all of us. That's nature's way of ensuring we perpetuate our species— by making some of them so fucking irresistible that we lose our minds." He looked down at his watch. "I have a meeting across town in a few minutes. I should head out." He gave Gio a pat on the back. "You'll survive this, Gio. Hang in there. At least it's not a brain tumor."

After Kane left, Gio sat at his desk and thought about what he'd said. Although he disagreed with the diagnosis his friend had given him, some of his advice had merit. If this were a business deal, nothing would stop him from closing on it.

It was only in his personal life that he held himself back. Deny. Control. Remember your duty. Keep emotions in check. Do nothing that risks the stability of the family or the company.

Julia endangered all that.

Around her, he didn't care about anything else.

And Rena was right: That had him shaking in his black Bruno Magli shoes.

"Rena, is Julia on tonight?"

"No, she called in sick."

His stomach flipped painfully. "Clear my schedule for today."

"Of course."

He didn't give himself time to second-guess his decision. He removed his tie and jacket and threw them on the chair before heading out of his office. As he walked by Rena's desk, he growled, "I'm not happy with you."

She smiled back at him. "I can live with that. Now go see what's wrong with Julia. I have a feeling it's the same thing that ails you."

୦୪

Still in her nightgown, with her hair sticking up wildly in all directions, Julia sat in the middle of her bed, hugging her knees. *I should throw the roses away. Keeping them is a constant reminder of the fool I made of myself.*

Gio hadn't called.

Not that I expected him to after how our date ended.

What did I think would happen? That we'd discover we had more in common than bits and pieces that are hot for each other? Was I expecting to wow him with witty dialogue? Floor him with my sophisticated banter?

That a bad decision could lead to something wonderful?

I'm such an idiot.

He has been honest about what he wants. I'm the one who keeps wavering and driving us both crazy. What did Mom used to say? "If you plant a potato, you get a potato." Julia used to roll her eyes at her mother whenever she'd say it. It was another way of saying, "If you go looking for trouble, you'll find it."

Or, if you date a man who says he's willing to pay you for sex—you end up feeling like a woman who was offered money for sex. Even if he wrapped the offer in a cushion of a thousand roses.

Or worse, you regret not saying yes, even though you hate yourself for wanting him enough to consider shelving your self-respect and giving in.

I can't keep calling in sick to Cogent.

But I can't watch him walk by me like I don't matter.

I'll quit tomorrow. Then I'll pick myself up, write a new résumé, find another night job, and get back out there. It'll be okay. This doesn't change anything.

She flipped on the television and searched until she found a sappy movie she knew would have her in tears. *I'll be strong again tomorrow. Right now, I'm going to let myself wallow.*

She reached for a box of tissues and lost herself in a story she'd watched a hundred times before, sobbing through scenes she knew well enough to mouth the words to, and hugged her pillow to her stomach as the heroine came to the same conclusion she had: *Men suck.*

A knock on her apartment door echoed through the room. She didn't have many friends in the city and most of them worked during the day. She knelt on her bed and looked at herself in the mirror. Yesterday's mascara was smudged beneath two bloodshot eyes. Her nose was red and puffy from crying. She scrambled to pick up the tissues that were scattered across her bed. "Who is it?" she called out.

The answer was concealed by the noise of the television. She turned it off and mentally smacked herself for saying anything. *I should have pretended I wasn't here. My television was on, though. So what? People leave them on all the time.*

Hastily wiping off any makeup she could, she put a bathrobe on over her nightgown and went onto her tiptoes to peer out the peephole.

Paul.

She turned and slumped against the door in relief, even as she tried to deny a wave of disappointment that it wasn't Gio. *He's not coming. Accept it.*

Julia unlocked the door and opened it, smiling when Paul held up a bag from the neighborhood deli. He was dressed in jeans a tight T-shirt that accentuated his enormous muscles. The sight should have been pleasurable, but seeing Paul only reminded Julia of how Gio had looked the first time she'd seen him. *Stop it.* She chastised herself for torturing herself with an image of someone she had no intention of ever seeing again.

Paul whistled appreciatively at the number of flowers that still filled every corner of the floor. Then he handed Julia the paper bag. "When you called in again, Tom and I started to worry. He asked me to come check on you. You look awful. Are you fighting what we had? Do you want me to run to the pharmacy?"

A quick peek into the bag revealed soup. "No, I'm fine," she said and burst into tears. Soup reminded her of how her mother had always taken care of her. Thinking of her mother made her feel even worse about moping over problems that were trivial by comparison. She wanted to call her mother to talk about Gio but knew she couldn't. She wanted to call Gio to talk about her mother, but that door was also closed. She suddenly felt very alone.

"Hey, hey, hey. Don't cry. I handle throwup much better than tears."

His comment made Julia laugh, even as tears continued running down her cheeks. "I'm not sick."

He reached out and drew her into his arms. His embrace nearly cut off her oxygen. "Come here." He hugged her tighter. "Is this about You Know Who?"

Julia sniffed and nodded, finding comfort in the warmth of her hulking friend's arms. "I know he is wrong for me, but I can't seem to control myself when I'm around him. It's like my brain shuts off. I'm quitting Cogent tomorrow, Paul. I hope it doesn't leave you guys short staffed. I can't go back there."

Paul set her back from him. "Hang on. I care, but I have to stop hugging you before I get a stiffie."

Julia's eyes widened and she burst out laughing, imagining what Tom would say if he were there. "Paul..."

He smiled unabashedly. "Hey, I'm human. Would you rather I tell you or let you feel it?"

A wave of laughter erupted from her, then quelled as a thought came to her. "I'm going to miss you."

"Are you sure you need to quit?"

"Yes."

"Did he hurt you?" Paul puffed up like a rooster preparing to defend one of his hens.

From behind Paul, through the still-open door, Gio's voice carried a deadly cold tone. "Well, this is an unexpected turn of events."

Initial embarrassment was replaced with anger. *I have nothing to feel embarrassed about.* "What are you doing here?"

Gio stepped into the small apartment, which suddenly felt claustrophobically small with the two large men circling each other. "The better question is, what is *he* doing here?"

Raising her chin defiantly, Julia said, "You don't have the right to ask."

Gio's eyes narrowed and his attention focused on Paul. "Don't you work for me?"

"Not until five o'clock," Paul answered in a tone that goaded Gio.

As the two of them squared off, Julia snapped, "He came by to make sure I was okay. Not that I owe you an explanation. You and I said everything we needed to say the other night."

Looking away from Julia to Paul, Gio said, "I refuse to discuss this in front of him."

Paul planted his feet. "I'm not leaving unless she tells me to go."

Although Julia appreciated the sentiment, she didn't want them both to lose their jobs because she'd sent Gio mixed messages. "I'm fine, Paul. Go. We'll talk later."

Reluctantly, Paul nodded. As he passed Gio, he knocked shoulder to shoulder with him aggressively. "Keep your hands to yourself. If I hear that you—"

Gio punched him square in the face and sent the man falling back against the wall, sinking down to the floor from the perfect hit and sending several vases spilling onto the carpet. Julia rushed to Paul's side. "Oh, my God. You broke his nose. It's bleeding."

Then she spun on Gio. "How could you? How could you hit him? He was only trying to protect me."

Gio was momentarily at a loss for words.

Paul pulled himself back up from the floor and wiped the blood on the sleeve of his T-shirt. "You want to try that again?"

Leaning in with a threat, Gio said, "If you touch me, I'll gladly send you to the floor a second time."

Julia wedged herself between the two of them. "Stop it. Stop it right now." She looked over her shoulder at her hulking friend and said, "Paul, I'll handle this. Don't get fired because of me."

"I'm not afraid of Mr. Fancy Pants."

"I know you're not, Paul, but Mr. Andrade's right. We do have to talk. And we can't do that with you here."

"If you're sure."

She looked at Gio's still-angry expression and nodded. *Mr. Fancy Pants doesn't scare me, either.* "I'm sure."

With one final glare at Gio, Paul walked out of the apartment.

Gio closed the door firmly, then turned to Julia. "I don't like the idea of you with another man."

Julia stood her ground. "Paul is not another man. Well, he is a man, but he's harmless. He brought soup."

Advancing on Julia, Gio said, "He wasn't here just because he thought you were sick." The desire in Gio's eyes sent a shiver of anticipation through Julia.

She took a step back and knocked over a vase. The water spilled onto her bare foot, reminding her she was still in her nightgown. "You didn't have to punch him."

"Yes, I did."

When her next step brought the back of her legs against the edge of her bed, she wrapped her bathrobe tighter around herself. "Why are you here, Gio?"

He didn't stop until only an inch separated them. A mere inch. Easily crossed and dangerously tempting. "You know why."

Squaring her shoulders, Julia met his eyes boldly. "You told me the other day that this wasn't a good idea."

He untied the belt of her bathrobe with one hand, whipped it free of its loops, and threw it behind him. "I changed my mind."

"And what if I haven't?" she whispered.

He eased the robe off her shoulders, dropping it to the floor and bending down to kiss her newly exposed collarbone. "Then tell me to leave."

She closed her eyes as every fiber of her body began to burn for him. "I can't," she admitted hoarsely. "I want you to stay."

He reached forward, grabbed the front of her thin nightgown, and tore it straight down the middle. Those rough hands turned gentle when they reached for her. He ran one hand reverently down her neck, across the swell of her breast, and down to possessively cup her sex. "I've never wanted a woman the way I want you, Julia." He slid a finger between her folds and captured her excited gasp with his mouth.

Julia opened herself to him. She clutched his chest as his hands explored her body. Their tongues danced and teased while his stroking became more intimate. His finger delved into her wet center while his mouth conquered hers. Stroke by stroke, he claimed her, enflamed her, brought her to a place where she was shaking with need.

Urgently, Julia fumbled to pull his shirt free of his trousers. She tore it open with the same enthusiasm he'd used to rip hers.

His free hand sought and worshipped her left nipple, twisting it lightly, then teasing the tip of it with his thumb. He was playing her body expertly, and she was helpless to resist the desire that whipped through her. She undid his belt and trousers, and sighed into his mouth with pleasure when her hands finally freed his rock-hard dick.

He was taking his time, even though he was clearly as excited by her as she was by him. His heart was beating wildly in his chest.

There was heady power in knowing he was as close to losing control as she was. Julia broke free from their kiss and nipped his muscular neck playfully. He groaned with pleasure, and Julia began to kiss her way down his chest. His hands came up to grip her head, but he didn't stop her.

She kissed her way down his flat stomach, dropped to her knees before him, and took him deeply into her mouth. His hands fisted in her hair. And still she took him deeper. His firm ass flexed beneath one of her hands while her other hand guided him in and out of her mouth.

She thought he would come in her mouth and she welcomed the idea, but he pulled out, stepped out of his pants, and threw her on her bed. The nightgown, still hanging from her shoulders like a cape, tangled beneath her. He reached into the pocket of his pants and, without taking his eyes off her, sheathed himself in a condom. He was beside her a moment later, rolling her on top of him and lowering her down onto him. He powerfully thrust upward, holding her by her hips as he did.

She sat up and threw her head back with a cry of pleasure. Although she was above him, he was in command now, driving into her, deeper and deeper with each thrust. She balanced on her knees and arched backward.

He sat up, pulled her forward and took one of her breasts into his hungry mouth while he raised and lowered her onto him. His teeth nipped her, then his hot tongue lapped each breast, a mix of pleasure and pain that sent Julia into writhing moans.

Rolling them both over, he took her hands and pinned them above her head, poising himself above her. He teased her by rubbing his tip over her clit while he watched her expression. "You're mine, Julia. Say it."

Even though she was practically sobbing for release, she couldn't say what he wanted to hear. Not without knowing what being his meant. She shook her head and closed her eyes.

He groaned in her ear and drove his shaft deeply into her with one powerful thrust. Julia welcomed him deeper and gave herself to the orgasm that swept through her as he continued to pound down into her. A moment later, he shuddered and came inside her.

He rolled onto his side and disposed of the condom, then pulled her back into his arms. They were both breathing hard. He buried his face in her hair and whispered, "You drive me crazy, Julia."

Naked and pressed up against the man she'd pined for all day, Julia chided him gently. "You think you're any better? I can't believe you hit Paul."

He took her chin in his hand and met her eyes seriously. "I don't want to talk about other men in your life."

Julia said, "It's not like that. I told you—"

Gio claimed her mouth with his and kissed her until she was squirming against him with need once again.

When the kiss ended, Julia slumped against Gio and laid her head on his chest. *Could he really be jealous of Paul?*

That would mean he cares about me, wouldn't it?

Or is this still about the crazy attraction between us?

What are we doing?

Oh, my God, why did I sleep with him? I should have told them both to leave.

"You're coming home with me," Gio said while he absently traced a hand down her bare back.

Raising herself up on one elbow, Julia said, "Didn't we already discuss this?"

He smiled devilishly and rolled her back so he was above her as he accepted her challenge. He claimed her mouth with his and held himself just above her, his hard dick nudging against her wet sex. His eyes burned with desire for her as he asked, "Do you have a condom in that drawer beside your bed?"

She'd never wanted to say yes so badly, but she didn't. "No."

Instead of being irritated by her answer, he arched himself off her and repositioned himself lower on the bed. He kissed the small swell of her stomach, then spread her legs wide and blew lightly on her exposed clit. "The only word I want you to say is 'yes.' "

Even though her body was humming with need for him, she shook her head. "No."

Holding her eyes with his, he spread her lower lips and licked her from back to front, lingering on her growing nub. His other hand slid beneath her to squeeze her ass possessively. "I'm going to enjoy changing your mind."

Julia clenched the comforter on either side of her as he plunged his tongue inside her, withdrew, then plunged in again. He rubbed her clit firmly with a rhythm that sent fire shooting through her. He blew lightly on her nub again. His tongue was everywhere while his fingers continued their war on her senses. He replaced his tongue with two fingers and found a spot that sent Julia out of her mind.

She cried out and thrashed against his hand. He held her easily and continued to pump his fingers in and out of her. When she was nearing climax, he stopped and looked up at her. "You know you want to say yes to me. Don't fight it. Give yourself to it."

He moved his fingers within her again, pausing to tug on her clit gently with his teeth, while never taking his eyes off her. "Say yes, Julia."

A wave of heat rose within Julia that consumed her. She came with her eyes open, staring into his dark ones while crying out, "Yes. Oh, yes. God, yes."

As she came back to earth, she thought, "What did I just agree to?" She realized she'd asked the question aloud as he rolled onto his back and lifted her so she was once again above him.

"Everything," he said with a lusty smile.

His answer sent a nervous thrill through her. *What is everything?*

He took one of her hands and wrapped it around his still throbbing erection. She didn't need more prompting than that.

I may not be up for everything.

But I'm down for this.

She eagerly took him in her mouth and took him to heaven.

∞

In the dark of her heavily flower-scented apartment, Gio held a naked, sleeping Julia in his arms and stared up at the ceiling. He couldn't remember a time in his adult life when he'd hit anyone. He didn't do that. He stayed in control.

Until Julia.

From the moment he'd decided to bring her to the wedding with him—an act that had been uncharacteristically impulsive—he'd become someone he didn't recognize. Emotion was best left out of most decisions. A cool head and determination equaled profit.

His philosophy hadn't made him a lonely man, as some might expect. He knew he wasn't a bad-looking man, but he was also jaded enough to realize that he could have been much less attractive and still gotten laid on a regular basis. Wealth did that. It was the ultimate aphrodisiac for enough women that he hadn't realized until he met Julia how bored he'd become with the predictability of it.

Julia was like a day of sunshine after years of rain. Everything about her felt good—too good.

Fucking her should have made me want her less.

I should be gathering my clothes and calling for my car. Instead, he pulled Julia closer against him. He looked around. The light in the miniscule bathroom illuminated the room enough for him to see the entire place from where he lay. One wall had a small cupboard, a portable stove top, and a microwave. A wooden chair and table were covered with small boxes.

A police car went by outside, the siren blaring loudly through the thin walls. He ran a hand absently down the back of her head and buried it in her long hair. *I don't even let women sleep over at my place—why do I think moving her in would work out?*

He looked down at her peaceful profile. *Because the alternative is leaving her here again, and that is not going to happen.*

She stirred against him. "Are you awake?" she whispered.

He ran his hand through her hair again. "Yes, and enjoying watching you sleep."

She stiffened. "I hope I wasn't drooling or anything."

He felt uncharacteristically lighthearted and joked gently, "Gentlemen don't wipe and tell."

She slapped his chest playfully. "That's awful. Funny, but awful."

He took her hand in his and brought it to his lips. "I don't have a reputation for being the nicest man. You'll have to get used to it."

She raised herself up on one elbow and looked down at him, gloriously unselfconscious about her nudity. "You say that like we... like we..."

He tucked a loose tendril behind her ear. "We?"

She looked down at him and chewed her bottom lip. "Tonight was wonderful, but it didn't change anything between us."

He pulled her back down against him. "I'd say it changed everything."

"What happened to us wanting completely different things?" she asked.

He leaned down and kissed her shoulder. "I'd say we've proven that theory wrong."

"I'm being serious."

"If you're hoping for a declaration of love, Julia, you're not going to get one. That's not who I am. But I want you beside me in my bed each night. I want to wake up to you. I can't stay away from you no matter how many times I tell myself I should. For now, let that be enough."

She closed her eyes and laid her head down on his chest. "I don't want you to buy me anything."

"I won't give you a goddamned thing. I promise."

She pinched his side lightly. "You're such an ass."

"But you're coming home with me."

"Yes," she said softly.

It was the sweetest word he'd ever heard.

Come Away with Me

Chapter Fourteen

JULIA CALLED IN her resignation the next day and no one seemed surprised. She'd done it during the day because she couldn't face Tom and Paul. She wasn't ready to answer the questions they'd ask.

Gio sent a driver over midmorning to pick her up and bring her to his apartment. It felt unreal handing his driver luggage as if she were going on a vacation. She couldn't meet the driver's eyes. *Does he know? Does he care? Has he done this a hundred times before?*

He grunted when he picked up her second case—the one that was full of her samples, her tools, and all of her magazines. *Hey, hey. Be careful with that. That's only my life in there.*

The drive to Gio's building uptown gave Julia far too much time to think. Through the car window, she studied the blur of pedestrians on the sidewalks and wondered what had brought each of them to New York.

How many of them reached their dreams? How many found themselves lost on tangents that distracted them long enough that their dreams slipped away?

The bellman met Julia at the curb and took her luggage with a smile. He led her to the elevator and rode with her, silently, to the top. The entire experience was surreal. An older man in a suit opened the door to Gio's apartment and introduced himself as Miles, the butler.

He brought Julia's luggage to Gio's bedroom and asked if she would like him to unpack for her. The question surprised Julia. He was about her father's age, and the idea of him unpacking her things made her uncomfortable.

"You do that?"

"Of course, Miss Bennett."

"But then you'd see all of my... stuff," she said and blushed.

A small smile stretched the man's lips. Blandly, he said, "Whatever you prefer. I don't mind."

"Because you're used to it?" She couldn't contain her curiosity. "*Are* you used to it? Does Mr. Andrade have many women stay here?"

"I really can't say," he said and took a step to leave. "If there is nothing you need I'll leave you to unpack."

Julia nodded in understanding. "You can't tell me because of some butler-boss confidentially agreement? Gotcha." She put one of her bags on the bed. "I didn't mean to make you uncomfortable with the question. I mean, does it matter anyway what the answer would have been? If you said that he'd had a hundred women live here already, what would I do—run? I know this isn't permanent. It's not even a good idea, really. It's just that he asked me when I was... when we were... I couldn't think. I should have stalled—given myself time to think this through. Because here I am now... wondering if I made the right choice."

Miles stopped at the door and turned back to look at her. "Miss Bennett?"

Julia raised a hand to stop him. "You don't have to say it. I shouldn't have asked. Don't risk losing your job by telling me anything."

"I was wondering if you were hungry."

Julia covered her eyes with one hand and wished she could disappear. "Oh. Yes. Food. No. I mean, no. I'm not hungry. Thank you." *Stop talking. Why did I think I could do this?*

Instead of immediately leaving, Miles cleared his throat and said, "I have worked for Mr. Andrade since his mid-twenties. You are the first woman who has ever brought luggage."

Julia lowered her hand. She didn't want to read too much into that information. "Really?"

With a slight incline of his head, Miles said, "I have also never made breakfast for anyone except Mr. Andrade."

Although there was nothing in Mile's expression to hint how he felt one way or another about her staying there, she was touched by what he'd revealed to her. "Thank you, Miles."

"You're welcome, Miss Bennett. Mr. Andrade had me clear out the other bedroom for you to use as a studio. Please tell me if you need any help setting it up."

He closed the door behind him, and Julia sat on the edge of the bed she knew she'd share with Gio that night. *A studio? For me?*

I don't need that unless I'm staying for a while.
Like, moving in.
Holy shit.
Did I just move in with Gio?

◌

Gio came home to Julia that night, and every night for the next week. Beyond the lovemaking, he enjoyed having her in his apartment. They fell into a comfortable pattern over the next week. They made love each night, woke early, and often made love again.

The more time he spent with her, the more he enjoyed the simple pleasures. Watching her wake in the morning. Wondering what she would say today that would make his unflappable butler turn away to hide a smile. Coming home and having someone to talk over his day with.

For the first time in his life, Gio found himself sharing stories about the project he was working on. He found Julia's ideas refreshing and often thought provoking. Although he wouldn't admit it to anyone, she was the reason he turned down the Atwater deal. There were other projects he could work on, ones that were less controversial, one he could be proud to discuss.

Her opinion mattered to him in a way that no one's had before. It both scared and inspired him. Just as she did.

Julia had meant what she'd said. She didn't want money from him. She didn't want gifts from him. Although she didn't immediately apply for another job, she used her time during the day to add to her jewelry line. Each night when he came home she had a new piece to show him, and a new story on how she had reached out to another jewelry store.

It would've only taken one call from him for her to make the sale. But she had made him promise not to make that call. She wanted to do this on her own. And for reasons he couldn't explain to himself, he wanted her to have that. He wanted her to know that she had done it on her own. The more they spoke, the more he understood the sale of the jewelry was as much about the journey as it was the money.

Gio didn't ask himself what the future held for them. He had her in his life, in his bed, and for now, that was enough.

Chapter Fifteen

JULIA STEPPED OUT of the apartment building one morning and watched a long black stretch limo pull up beside her. *Maddy again?*

The back window rolled down and an older woman with dark brown hair done up in a sophisticated chignon waved for Julia to approach the limo. Everything about her said refined sophistication. Julia looked over her shoulder and then pointed at her own chest in question.

The beautiful older woman nodded impatiently, and Julia walked over. *Maybe she's lost and needs directions to some charity event?*

"Julia Bennett?"

"Yes?" Julia answered in confusion. "Do I know you?"

"No, but I know you, and we need to talk." The driver came around and opened the limo door for Julia to enter.

Julia looked back and forth from the Cogent Solutions building ahead to the dark interior of the vehicle. "I have an appointment I need to get to this morning. I can't be late."

The woman leaned out and gave a small smile. "This will only take a few minutes and could be quite a lucrative opportunity for you."

"You're interested in my jewelry?"

"I don't discuss business in the street," she said coldly and sat back in the limo.

They say opportunity knocks. No one ever mentioned that it could pull up beside you in a limo. *Am I crazy to think about getting in? My life is already so off course.*

On the other hand, if I don't get in, I will never know what she might have offered me. For all I know, she is an eccentric gem collector and wants me to create the perfect pieces to showcase her stones.

Or she's a high-paid madam, and this is how she recruits.

Julia remembered the harsh lines on the older woman's face and thought, *No, she looks way too uptight to have had sex in the last decade.*

What kind of a businesswoman am I if I won't even listen to a proposal?

Julia slid into the limo and tried not to jump when the driver closed the door behind her. Her hands went suddenly cold when the vehicle pulled out into traffic. "Where are we going?"

The woman's smile didn't reach her eyes. "We'll merely circle the block."

Of course. How silly of me to worry.

I really have to stop getting into limos with people I don't know.

"I've done research on you since I first heard about you. Have you sold any of your jewelry yet? Made any noteworthy connections?"

"I have some leads," Julia said vaguely. *Don't show your hand in negotiations. She must have heard about me from one of the entrepreneurs I showed my line to.* A burst of excitement started to build in her stomach. *Persistence does pay off. My name is out there. This could be it.*

"You must be getting anxious about your father's company. Your time is running out to save it, isn't it?"

The hair on the back of Julia's neck rose. *I never mention that while I pitch.* "I'm sorry, what did you say your name was again?"

"I didn't," the woman said, flashing another smile that did little to calm Julia's nerves. "Who I am is irrelevant." She took out an envelope and tossed it onto Julia's lap. "What matters is that I am willing to pay you to go home to your family."

Julia opened the thick envelope and looked back at the woman in confusion.

"It's one hundred thousand dollars. You'll receive another hundred thousand once you've left New York and are back in Rhode Island."

Julia's mouth dropped open. "I don't understand."

"That is how much you need, isn't it?"

Shaking her head, Julia asked, "Yes, but I'm confused. Do you want me to work on my jewelry back in Rhode Island?"

"Keep your trinkets, dear. Just get the hell out of New York."

Julia's hand closed tightly on the envelope as she studied the woman's features, and an awful realization came to her. "Are you Gio's mother?"

"The resemblance is strong, no?"

Only in the worst possible way. You both assume I can be bought. "Why would you want me to leave New York?" Understanding hit her like a sledgehammer to the stomach. She held up the money, outraged heat spreading up her neck. "Are you upset that I'm living with him?"

"George isn't serious about you. You're the flavor of the month. Take the money. It'll last a lot longer than whatever you think you have with him. All I ask is that you leave before the weekend."

Julia couldn't remember ever being so insulted. "I'm not going anywhere. Well, I am going somewhere. I mean, we are. We're going to a wedding. Not ours."

"Perhaps you think I'm kidding? I couldn't be more serious." An ugly expression darkened the woman's face. "How much does your father's company mean to you? You can save it, and no one ever needs to know how you did it. Tell me, are a few romps with my son worth watching your family lose everything?"

Her words sent a chill down Julia's back. She laid the envelope down on the seat beside her and reached for the door handle. "It's not like that. And my father's company is going to be fine. I still have time to make a sale."

"If you're counting on my son to give you money, he won't. A week from now he won't even remember you."

Julia hastily climbed out of the limo. *That's quite a family you have there, Gio.*

Holy shit.

Instead of taking the bus down to the Diamond District, Julia called and rescheduled her appointment. She knew she couldn't tell Gio what had happened, but she needed to see him.

❧

Tom glared at her when she entered the building. She walked over to the security station.

She looked at the stranger sitting next to him and asked, "Where's Paul?" Guilt struck Julia when she realized that she'd been so swept away by Gio that she hadn't called Paul to check on him. *I've always believed that the right match made you a better version of yourself. I'm so absorbed in what's going on with Gio, I didn't think about Paul. What does that mean? Is Gio the wrong man for me, or would I be an ass regardless of who I'm with?*

Tom put the clipboard down decisively. "Where do you think he is? Your boyfriend fired him."

Julia frowned. "No."

Tom glared at her again. "I knew you'd be trouble from the first time I saw you. You couldn't just do your job, could you?"

Julia wished the floor would open and swallow her up. She felt horrible that she'd played a role in separating them. She'd spent enough time with both of them to know that loss was the source of Tom's anger. He would miss working with his best friend. "I'll talk to Gio... Mr. Andrade. I'll fix this."

"You've done enough. Paul's still looking for a job. He doesn't interview well."

Despite Tom's angry tone, Julia leaned closer. "I am sorry. I didn't mean for this to happen. You know that."

Her words softened Tom's expression slightly. "I told Paul to check on you. I guess it's partially my fault."

"There has to be something I can do."

Gio was a reasonable man. Was it too late to ask Gio to hire Paul back?

Rena was at her desk when Julia entered Gio's outer office. "Is he in?" Julia asked tentatively.

Rena stepped out from behind her desk. "He is. How are you?"

"Good," Julia said, straightening her shoulders in determination. "Could you tell him that I'm here?"

Instead of reaching for her phone, Rena looked her over. "Are you still going to the wedding with him?"

"Yes, is that a problem?" Julia asked cautiously. *Seriously? And they say people in small towns can't mind their own business? This is ridiculous.*

Rena's eyebrows rose in reaction to Julia's tone. "I was wondering if you felt ready."

"Ready?"

"Have you looked over the invitation list? You should wear your own jewelry when you go. Who knows, you may find an investor. If you'd like, I could help you recognize who's who."

It was hard not to be suspicious of the kind offer. Julia wasn't about to be fooled twice in one day. "Why would you do that?"

"I like you?" When Julia looked unconvinced, Rena added, "How about, because I have the feeling that if our roles were reversed you would help me?"

Julia let her suspicions fall away. Rena had never given her a reason not to trust her. And it wouldn't hurt to go into the situation as prepared as possible. *I used to think I liked surprises. I'm not finding that as true in this situation.* "I have to ask Gio something, but then, yes, I'd like to talk to you about what to expect tomorrow."

"Great. If you don't have your dress yet, I know the perfect place to look for one."

A dress? Of course I need a dress. Shit. "Thank you for the offer, but I can wear the one I just bought."

"No, that one has been in the papers. You need something new." Rena went back to her desk, sat down, and picked up her phone. "Julia is here to see you. Yes, I'll send her right in, but before I do... one quick question. Do you mind if I take her dress shopping tonight and charge it to you? That's what I thought." She hung up and smiled at Julia. "All set. He told me to have you back early." Rena winked at Julia. "I personally think you should make him cool his heels waiting for you. He's far too used to getting what he wants."

"I don't need another dress. I don't want him to buy me anything," Julia said adamantly.

Rena stood and crossed to stand near her. "Whoa. I'm sorry. I just assumed..."

"That I'm with him for what I can get from him?"

Rena raised her hands in truce. "No, that you'd want something new for a high-profile wedding, and that since he invited you I figured he should buy it for you."

"Well, I don't, and he shouldn't."

"Hey," Rena said gently, "my family drags me to so many social events I have a closet full of dresses I'll never wear again. You could borrow a couple."

Releasing her breath slowly, Julia searched Rena's face. "If you're sure."

A wide smile spread across Rena's face. "We'll make a girls' night of it."

"I'd like that."

"Julia," Gio said from the doorway. She thanked Rena one last time and crossed the office to Gio. He closed the door and locked it behind her, taking her mouth passionately as if they'd been apart far longer than the few hours they'd had been separated. She wrapped her arms around his neck and gave herself fully to the moment.

When he broke off the kiss, he touched his forehead to hers, still holding her in his arms. "I thought having you at my place would make it easier for me to concentrate, but I find myself watching the clock." He claimed her mouth again and Julia shuddered against him with pleasure. "You're one powerful addiction."

She could have said the same. A moment in his presence and nothing else mattered. *Want me on the desk? Let me scramble on up there. How about the couch? The carpet? I don't care who knows what we're doing or who walks in. I want you on me, in me, licking whatever you want to. Just don't stop.*

He raised his head, breathing as raggedly as she was. "Sorry, I lose my head around you. Did you come to see me for a reason, or just for this?" The lusty smile he gave her sent heat rushing through her. "Either is fine with me."

Julia put a shaky hand up to her kiss-swollen mouth. *Did I come here for a reason?*

You know, besides this?

She shook her head to clear it. *I know I'm forgetting something.*

He looped his hands behind her and pulled her full against the evidence of his arousal. "I like that you get along with Rena, but you don't need a dress for the wedding. I have no intention of going anymore."

Julia pulled back. "Why?"

"It doesn't matter."

"It matters to me." Julia realized that although they had spoken about many things over the last week, he had avoided all personal topics. "We said we were going. They're expecting us. Maddy will be hurt if we don't show up."

"I've made my decision."

"Without even talking to me about it?"

"It's my family."

"And none of my business," she said, unable to keep some of the hurt she felt out of her voice.

His silence was his answer.

Julia stepped out of his embrace. He didn't try to stop her, and that confused her even more. Was his mother right—at least when it came to how temporary their union was? Julia didn't feel like the flavor of the month. What they had felt special. *But maybe that's how he makes every woman feel?*

In that moment of resistance, she remembered part of why she'd come to see him. "About Paul."

Gio frowned. "Why are we still talking about that man?"

She looked him in the eye and said, "I didn't know you fired him. I understand that he went too far, but he was protecting me. I feel awful that he lost his job over me. He and Tom have been friends forever. I can't be the reason they don't work together anymore."

Gio returned to his desk and sat down, a not-so-subtle act of dismissal. "Was there something else you wanted?"

Julia glared at him. "Sometimes I don't like you very much."

He was around his desk with a predatory swiftness and harshly pulled her against him. "You don't have to like me." He dug a hand into her hair and held her immobile before him. "You want me." Julia wanted to hate the way he took her mouth in his as if she belonged to him, but the strength of him was heady. She welcomed his plundering kiss and reveled at how he also lost control. He lifted her and carried her toward the couch.

The intercom on his desk beeped, then his secretary's voice filled the room. "I'm ready when Julia is. We have a car waiting for us downstairs."

Gio groaned. "Why does she hate me? Do I not pay her enough?" He let Julia's feet slide to the ground.

Julia adjusted her clothing and gathered her thoughts. Gio was a strong man and one who was painfully honest, but he wasn't cruel. And he cared about her; she had to believe that. "I'm going out with Rena tonight. She said she had some dresses that might fit me."

"Dresses for a wedding we're not attending?"

Julia put a hand on one hip. "Yes."

"Why borrow from her? I said she could take you shopping." Julia met his eyes angrily and his expression darkened. "Because you don't want anything from me."

In that moment, Julia glimpsed the reason she couldn't stay away from him. However he tried to hide it, she knew he felt things deeply. "I do want something from you, but nothing you could buy."

He had a cornered look in his eyes that reminded her of the stray dog her family had once brought in during a snowstorm when Julia was twelve. The dog had paced and clawed at the door as if he were trapped in the shelter they had offered him. He'd responded to attempts to pet him with defensive snarls. Her mother had suggested that they call the dog warden. They didn't need a dog and certainly not one who might be a danger. Her father had asked them both to give him a month. He said the dog didn't become fearful in a day, and expecting him to trust them that quickly was unrealistic.

Her father had taken a bowl of food and put it on the porch. Before he opened the door to let the dog out, he'd bent and looked into the dog's eyes and said calmly, "You're a good dog, and this can be your home if you want it."

She and her mother had expected the dog to run off into the snow.

Julia smiled as she remembered how her mother had gently teased her husband by asking, "Did he answer you?"

Her gentle giant of a father had merely shrugged and said, "His actions will be his answer."

Rodin, as they'd come to call him, became her father's loyal shadow. He never did sleep in the house, but he met her father on the porch each morning and went with him to his furniture factory. For her father, he'd allowed the vet to give him annual shots as long as the vet came to the house. When he died, the family had buried Rodin in a plot behind the factory, beneath the tree where he'd always spent the day waiting for her father to finish work so he could walk him home.

Julia wondered what Gio would think of the comparison. The more she got to know him, the more she sensed that he needed shelter from his own storm.

Just as much as he needed someone to believe in him.

He might pretend he didn't care what she thought of him, but she wasn't fooled. *He'll do the right thing.* Julia went up onto her tiptoes and gave him a quick kiss before heading toward the door. She left him standing in the middle of his office shaking his head.

❧

Gio dropped back into his office chair with a groan. As he always felt after Julia left, Gio felt off balance.

He called his friend Kane and told him that it was time for him to repay him for all the years that Rena had worked for him. He gave Kane Paul's name and information and asked him to hire him. He also explained that Paul might come as a package deal with another man. Both had good work histories with his company, but for personal reasons he preferred they work elsewhere. He called down to Tom and explained the offer to him. Although he refused to hire Paul back, he wanted Julia to be happy.

One woman's opinion shouldn't matter so much to him.

But there was no denying that it did.

His cell phone rang. He checked caller ID and his mood soured more. "Mother," he said coolly.

"George, tell me you're not attending the Andrade wedding on Isola Santos. I'm surprised your uncles have the nerve to invite anyone there." Her dislike of the possibility was clear in her tone.

He almost reassured her he wasn't. Having Julia in his life had brought him a sense of contentment he had decided not to let ancient history threaten. Why look for answers in the past when he had everything he needed right there beside him every night?

Some doors were better left closed.

His mother hadn't hidden her concern when she'd heard he and his brothers had attended a function with the family over the summer, but she'd settled down when nothing came from it.

Patrice Andrade, or, as she was once again known, Patrice Stanfield, daughter of one of the wealthiest oil families in the United States, wasn't known for being an emotional woman. She had even less tolerance for dramatics in others.

Which made her escalating agitation over the wedding difficult to dismiss. It begged the question: *Why?*

Is it the island she hates, or the idea that we may reconcile with our father's family?

He answered vaguely, "I told them I would."

"How could you, Gio? With everything you know?"

"It's a wedding. Nothing more."

"But why are you going? They've invited you to weddings before. You've never gone. Are you hoping things will be different? They won't be. Remember what they've taken from you."

She'd voiced that sentiment a hundred times before. He'd thought himself immune to it, but this time it brought back anger he hadn't known was still within him. "How could I forget with you around to remind me?"

His mother's voice softened. "You're better than them, George. They did you a favor when they showed you how they really felt. You don't need them."

Gio let out a relieved breath. "Is this the only topic you called to discuss? Because I have a meeting waiting for me." Which was partially true. Somewhere in the world some executive was waiting for him to return his call.

"I saw you in the papers chasing after some woman. Making a fool of yourself in public undermines the company's image."

"Good-bye, Mother."

Just before he hung up, she said, "Watch your brothers on the island, George. Don't let your uncles manipulate them. They lie as easily as they breathe."

How many times had they had this very conversation? Looking up at the ceiling in frustration, Gio said, "We're not little boys anymore. You don't have to protect us from them."

"You're wrong, George. I just hope you realize that before they tear our family apart in a way that even you can't fix."

She hung up.

Tear us apart?

I'd say that happened a long time ago.

Her call had changed his mind about seeing his father's family again, and not in the way his mother had hoped. He was certain now he had to go. He needed to know what awaited him that his mother feared.

But unlike the first time he'd decided to attend the wedding, he didn't want to bring Julia with him. If the situation got ugly, he wanted her far away from it.

❀

Rena's Queen Anne townhouse in Henderson Place had surprised Julia. Even to someone as new to New York as Julia was, the rare cul-de-sac neighborhood implied expensive and exclusive. And if Rena's designer wardrobe was any indication, the area's high price hadn't affected her ability to shop.

Which should have made Julia feel uncomfortable, but Rena had a down-to-earth personality. As she encouraged her to try on dress after dress, Julia felt like she was with her friends back in Rhode Island preparing for prom. They laughed their way through good and bad fits.

While standing before the mirror in a navy strapless Gucci gown that fit her perfectly, Julia met Rena's eyes in the mirror and asked, "How long have you known Gio?"

Rena smiled and looked up at the ceiling as if counting the years in her head. "I was still in braces when we first met. My brother, Kane, has been his best friend since middle school."

A sliver of uncertainty crept into Julia. "Gio hasn't mentioned him to me, but there is a lot he doesn't tell me."

Rena came to stand beside Julia in front of the mirror. Simply for the fun of it, she was dressed in a whimsical ultrafitted nude gown that boasted not only a bustier but also a long skirt covered in a layer of feathers. She said she'd fallen in love with it when she'd seen it on a runway in London but hadn't yet found an event to wear it to. "Give him time. Gio doesn't trust people easily. He's had good reason not to."

Julia couldn't contain her question. "What happened?"

Rena smiled regretfully. "I wish I could tell you. I'm not supposed to know. He'd kill Kane for telling me."

Changing the subject, Julia looked down at her own dress and said, "Will I need this dress? He said we're not going to the wedding anymore."

"He'll go. He may say he doesn't care about his cousins, but he does. He always has." She took one of Julia's hands in hers. "Take the dress, and don't give up on him. He needs someone like you."

Julia met her own eyes in the mirror.

I want to believe that.

I desperately want to believe that.

Several hours later, Julia followed Gio's driver as he carried the bags of dresses and shoes Rena had loaned her. Although it was still strange having someone always at her side anticipating her needs, she had to admit it was nice.

It still feels like a dream.

Gio opened the door of his apartment and Julia's heart pounded wildly in her chest. His eyes were dark and burning with need for her. *If this is a dream, wake me tomorrow.*

She flew into his arms and met his kiss eagerly. He picked her up and carried her to the bedroom. He sat on the edge of his bed and simply held her for a moment, breathing in the scent of her hair like he'd waited all day to do just that.

She pulled her head back and looked up at him. There was sadness in his eyes that made her want to throw her arms around him and comfort him. "What's wrong?"

"I've decided to attend the wedding this weekend. I leave on Friday morning."

"You leave?"

He put a hand beneath her chin and raised her face up so she would meet his eyes. "You're not coming with me."

Julia clasped her suddenly cold hands in front of her. "Why?" *Because it's over? This can't be how it ends. We haven't even fought.* "You wanted me to go. What's changed?"

He slid her off him and stood. "I no longer want you there."

Confused, Julia stood straight and tall in front of him. "I don't believe you."

"I don't know how to be clearer."

She stepped closer and studied his expression. Questions clamored within her. Insecurities circled like vultures waiting to swoop in. Rena's words came back to her, bolstering her resolve. *Don't give up on him.* "How about just being honest?"

He lashed out verbally. "Dammit, Julia. I'm not taking you to the wedding. I refuse to involve you in this."

Tears clouded Julia's eyes as she saw what was behind his anger. He wanted to protect her. "Okay."

He frowned down at her. "Why aren't you upset?"

Julia's throat clogged with emotion. "Because I'm listening with my heart and not my ears. My father taught me that. It's how he said you see the soul of something. You close out all distractions and you let yourself feel the essence of it." She took him by the hand and led him out of the bedroom to one of the couches in the living room. She sat down even when he continued to stand and glower down at her. "You're angry, but not at me. Let's start over. Yell and rant as much as you want. Let it out. Then we'll talk."

Gio shook his head in bewilderment. "What?"

"Throw something if it makes you feel better. Sometimes I do that. Bottling it up only makes it worse."

"I don't yell."

"Everyone yells."

He shook his head again.

"Then I'll do it for you." She let out a high-pitched angry scream.

He sat beside her. "What are you doing? Stop."

She screamed again.

He covered her mouth. "Someone is going to call the police."

She smiled beneath his hand. He removed it and she said, "I just released all the anger I felt when you told me I couldn't go to the wedding. Now you do it. You'll feel better."

He cocked his head to one side, then started to laugh. He laughed so hard his eyes misted over. And while he did he pulled her into his arms and hugged her.

She nodded with approval. "Laughter works, too. How do you feel?"

He cupped her face between both of his hands and looked down at her, his expression sobering. "Better than I have in a long, long time."

"Do you want to talk now?

"Hell no."

Even though she was disappointed, she was relieved to see him smiling. He swung her up and over one of his shoulders. "I just thought of another way to relieve some of my stress."

She playfully swatted his back. "Don't think this lets you off the hook. I want to know why you don't want to take me to the wedding."

He growled and rolled onto the bed with her. "What's it going to take for you to stop talking?"

Julia smiled up at him impishly. "Do I really need to tell you?"

She didn't.

The next hour left her pleasantly unable to speak or even form a coherent thought.

Chapter Sixteen

JULIA WOKE IN Gio's arms. Lying naked in his embrace was heaven. He was absently tracing the curve of her lower back.

She hugged him tightly. She wanted to ask him so many questions, but she held her tongue. He would tell her when he was ready. "Gio?"

"Hmmm?" he asked, resting his chin on the top of her head.

"I care about you."

He instantly tensed but said nothing. *What is he afraid I'll say? Who taught him that words of kindness are followed by something unpleasant?*

Rubbing her hand across his lightly haired chest, Julia said, "That's all. I just needed to say it."

He buried his face in her hair and held her for a moment longer, relaxing beneath her touch. "Did you have fun with Rena?"

Julia knew he was trying to distract her and she let him. "Yes. We even looked at some old photographs. I'm so jealous. How did you not have a gangly, awkward stage?"

He chuckled softly and ran his hand through her long hair. "I'm not sure I should let the two of you become friends."

"Too late," Julia said with a mischievous grin. "I love that she's your best friend's little sister. She told me that you and Kane ruled your high school. What was it like being so popular?"

Instead of laughing at her ribbing, his face grew serious. "Kane was my friend. The rest of them were more interested in how much money my family had. That's the problem with money. People don't see you. They see the car you drive. They see the house you live in. Beyond that, none of it is real. When you have enough money, it's no longer a thrill to get more of it. All that matters is keeping it and ensuring it's there for the next generation."

Julia held up one of her hands and rubbed her thumb and index finger together back and forth quickly. She stopped and said cheekily, "Do you know what that is? It's the world's smallest violin, and I'm playing it for your very sad story. Too much money. The burden of it. How did you survive?"

He raised his hand and slapped her bare ass with enough force that she jumped, but not enough to hurt her. "I thought you were a sweet woman."

She smiled back, unrepentant. "I am, but I call bullshit when I see it."

"That can be a dangerous trait," he said with a bit more seriousness. "Many people don't like having their reality challenged."

She propped herself up on one elbow and said, "I'm a lot tougher than you think."

He ran a gentle hand down one side of her face and down her neck. "Are you?"

"Yes, I am."

A pained expression twisted his face. "I don't know what the wedding will be like. It has the potential to become an ugly situation."

Julia leaned forward and rested her head on his chest. "Then you should definitely take me. You shouldn't go to something like that alone."

He shuddered beneath her, and Julia knew she'd said exactly what he needed to hear.

Chapter Seventeen

IT WAS A few minutes before three on Friday morning when they arrived at the private airfield. "Oh, hell no," Gio said as his town car pulled onto the tarmac next to his plane and he saw the outline of three men standing next to a stretch limo talking. "I told Rena to hire a second plane for them."

Julia leaned over him to look out the window. The move tightened the material of her slacks over the curve of her ass in the most tempting way. As adorable as she looked in them, he'd spent the ride over imagining taking them off her in the seclusion of the plane. "Who are they?" she asked.

"My brothers. They'll have to find their own damn plane."

"Won't they think it's strange that we don't want them to come with us?"

Gio raised his eyebrows and Julia turned an adorable shade of pink. "I don't care."

Julia said softly, "I'd like to meet them."

Gio swore beneath his breath. He still wasn't sure how he felt about Julia, but he knew damn well how he felt about sharing a six-hour flight with her and his brothers. He was about to explain to her why his way was the only way when he looked into her blue eyes and lost his resolve. "Nick will probably make a pass at you," he warned. "Even if I threaten to kill him for it."

"I'll laugh it off."

"Luke will bore you with details of his last surgery."

Julia turned so she was straddling Gio's lap, facing him. "I have the perfect game face for boring stories. Watch." She smiled at him and widened her eyes as if fascinated in what he was saying. "I look them straight in the eye and daydream away. It works every time."

Gio shook his head, losing the battle against her charm. "I'll have to remember that expression the next time I'm telling you something."

"I probably shouldn't have shared that," Julia said with a guilty grin, then peered out the window again. "What about your third brother?"

"Max? He's a wild card. I'm surprised he's here at all. He's not big on family events."

"They sound nice."

Giving in to the temptation of having her poised above him, he slid his hand between her legs and enjoyed watching her eyes half close with pleasure. "Not as nice as flying over alone would be."

Julia gave him a deep kiss, then murmured, "How about if I promise to make it up to you on the island? We'll sneak off somewhere during the reception. There has to be some private corner on it."

He savored the feel of her lips against his and considered her proposal.

She kissed him quickly and moved playfully away from him. "Unless you're not interested."

"Oh, I'm interested." He reached for her, but before he made contact the door of his town car opened.

Nick greeted them first. He bent to inspect the contents of the vehicle, then straightened and turned to speak to the brothers who stood behind him. "Luke was right. Gio brought a date. So, why couldn't I bring mine?"

Luke's sarcasm was thick. "You didn't know her name."

"It's a long flight. We would have figured it out."

Gio stepped out of the vehicle and faced the trio. He momentarily blocked the door behind him. "I wasn't aware we were traveling together."

Luke nodded. "I had Rena cancel our plane. It doesn't make sense for us to go separately."

His youngest brother, Max, came over and clapped a hand in greeting on Gio's shoulder. "Don't be cross with Luke. He clings to the possibility of reuniting the family."

Countering his brother, Nick asked, "But not you, Max? Why are you here if you don't care how it turns out?"

Max smiled. "I've run the odds in my head of one of you getting into a serious altercation on the island, and the probability is high."

Luke looked at him and raised one doubtful eyebrow. "And you're coming to make sure that doesn't happen?"

"Hell no, I don't want to miss it," Max said with a wicked grin only the youngest child could master.

Gio let out an audible sigh. "This isn't going to work." He half turned to climb back into his car, but Luke stopped him with a hand on his arm.

"Don't go, Gio. I wasn't screwing with you. I think it's important that we arrive together."

Gio looked back and forth between Julia's expectant expression and Luke's earnest one. He put his hand out to Julia, helping her out of the car. "This is Julia Bennett. She was raised in a nice family. Can we be on our best behavior for the next six hours?"

Nick leaned in and whistled appreciatively. "Is she the one who worked in the security department? She is hot. No wonder you broke your rule to date her. But seriously, am I the only one who recognizes a pattern at Cogent? Have you seen the new IT girl? She can fix my laptop anytime."

The group collectively held its breath as Gio's temper rose. His grip on Julia's hand tightened. To his surprise, Julia stepped forward and offered her other hand to Nick. "That's funny. A little inappropriate for the first time you meet me, but flattering if I overlook that last part."

Max laughed out loud. "I am definitely glad I decided to come."

Nick shook Julia's hand, then looked over at Gio. "You finally found a girl with a personality. Hallelujah. Watch out, though. She may give you one. I hear they're catching."

Max laughed again. "Are you going to let him get away with that, Gio?"

The trouble with his decision to cut the darker emotions out of his life was how it had left Gio feeling empty. He wanted to be hopeful like Luke, or laugh along with Max, but he couldn't. He and Nick had something in common. They were both broken in their own way. Instead of rising to Max's bait, Gio looked at his watch and said, "We told them we'd be there for tonight's party. We should get going." He motioned for his driver to put their bags on the plane.

The small Embraer Legacy business jet taxied down the private runway. All five of them sat in one main area, facing each other. Julia was more interested in looking out the window than at the luxurious details of the multimillion dollar aircraft. She took Gio's hand in hers. "I love flying. I haven't visited many places, but the ones I've seen have all been amazing. So flying, to me, means an adventure is beginning. Thank you for letting me come with you."

Her innocent enthusiasm pulled at a part of Gio he'd long considered dead. He leaned down and nuzzled her neck before he realized what he was doing. When he saw Nick's mouth drop open in shock, Gio raised his head and glared at all of his brothers.

After a moment of awkward silence, Luke said, "If you mess this up, Gio, you deserve to grow old alone."

Gio shook his head in denial. "We're not..." He almost said *serious,* but he looked down into Julia's trusting blue eyes and bit off the rest of his sentence.

I told her I'm not capable of love, but she doesn't believe that, does she?

One of us is wrong.

CB

Watching the Andrade brothers talk was more fascinating than any in-flight movie could have been. They all had dark hair, near-black eyes, and light olive skin. It was easy to tell they were brothers, but they were also very different. Julia studied each of them intently and listened with her heart.

Gio dressed in a classic style. Although all four were over six feet, Gio was the most intimidating of them. His features were harsher and his face most prone to frowning. He seemed to fill more space on the plane, and when he spoke his tone held a rigid authority. He was a walking ball of tension. Like a soldier asked to stand guard through the night, he never relaxed. *Who are you protecting, Gio? What are you so afraid people will find out?*

Nick had boyish good looks that he cultivated with expensive international flair. He belonged on a cover of GQ, with a drink in one hand, a woman on his arm, and a cocky expression on his face. Still, he shared a sad character trait with Gio: When he smiled, it didn't reach his eyes. *Do you know why Gio isn't happy? Is that what keeps you together but apart?* Every once in a while, Nick would look at Gio with anger burning in his eyes, even as he kept his tone light and joking. *What is it you can't forgive him for?*

Luke was every bit as striking in his good looks as his older brothers, but he dressed to play it down. He wore jeans and a polo shirt. He was the peacemaker of the family. Gio had said he was a doctor, and Julia could see why it was his calling. He listened when his brothers spoke, and his love for them was evident in everything he said to them. He seemed excited about attending the wedding in a way that none of his brothers were. *He doesn't know.*

Max had a bit of all of them in him. He was tough around the edges like Gio. He dressed to impress with expensive clothing tailored to fit him, and every now and then he would poke fun at one of his brothers in a way that was almost playful. Gio had nailed him when he'd called him a wild card. Julia didn't know what his motivation for coming was, but she didn't believe that it was the same as he'd said. He didn't appear to have ill feelings toward any of them. *If he knows, he'd never tell.* Gio said Max owned and developed casinos around the world. She could see that. *He plays his cards close to his chest.*

None of them mentioned their mother. Having met her, Julia wasn't surprised, but still, she thought it was sad they were heading off to a large family event and not one had suggested she should be there.

Before she thought it through, she asked aloud, "Where's your father?"

All conversation died. Although he didn't look happy about it, Gio bent toward her and explained quietly. "My father passed away years ago."

"I'm sorry to hear that. The wedding we're going to is for the son of one of his brothers?"

"Yes, my father was the oldest of three. The youngest of them, Victor Andrade, had one son—Stephan."

"And Maddy?"

Luke jumped in. "Maddy is Uncle Alessandro's daughter. She's married to an amazing French chef. If he offers to cook you anything—I mean anything—just say yes."

"I had the..." Julia stopped and decided to be less than completely honest, "pleasure of meeting Maddy. She was unexpectedly... welcoming."

"Maddy is certainly a character." Luke laughed, then grew more serious. "She keeps me up to date with that side of the family. They've had a rough time the last few years. That's one of the reasons she's determined to mend the rift in the family."

Gio released his seat belt and stretched his legs out before him. "Don't build this up into something it isn't, Luke. I, for one, have no intention of seeing any of them again after this weekend."

Nick left his seat to pour himself a Scotch from a crystal decanter.

Max leaned forward and asked, "Weren't you and Stephan close at one time?"

"No," Gio answered succinctly. "Nick was. He and Stephan toured the global party circuit together, both believing the tedious idea of working belonged to the generation who had created the family business. Stephan outgrew that phase."

Nick downed his glass in one shot and poured himself another. "We can't all be you, Gio. The perfect son. The perfect businessman. Completely lacking in conscience."

Gio stood slowly, his muscles flexing angrily as he did. "Stop drinking now, Nick, before you make a fool of yourself."

Nick downed the second glass defiantly. "Or what? What would you do?"

Gio walked over and took the crystal decanter from the counter. As calmly as if he were merely picking up something he'd dropped, he smashed the container on the corner of the bar, then dropped the ragged top to the carpeted floor with the rest of the shattered glass and alcohol. In a controlled, cool voice he said, "Whatever is necessary to protect the family."

Nick leaned down just as calmly, opened a door of the cabinet, took out another bottle, and placed it next to his glass. "There are at least ten more in there. How many will you break? Which one will convince you what I do is none of your goddamn business?"

Luke was out of his seat and between them. "Nick, enough."

Nick turned on Luke angrily. "How far would he have to go for you to judge him? If he threw me from the plane, would you justify even that? Or would you finally find the balls to confront him?"

Max leaned over to Julia and said, "Which one do you think would actually get ejected from the plane if it came to that? My money is on Luke. It's always the one in the cross fire that gets nailed."

Gio ignored his youngest brother's comment and said, "Go ahead and drink yourself into a stupor, Nick. Make a fool of yourself in front of everyone. Just stay the hell away from me while you do it."

Nick looked over at Julia and opened his mouth to say something more, but Luke took him by the arm and guided him away from the bar to the small kitchen area near the front of the plane. "Come on, let's make coffee. I don't care if you want it, I need some."

Max raised an eyebrow at his oldest brother. "That was extreme, Gio. You couldn't have made your point without making the entire plane smell like a distillery?"

"I went exactly as far as I had to," Gio said coldly. He turned and walked to the other side of the plane where their bags were stored.

Watching the exchange between the brothers was heartbreaking for Julia. She wanted to yell for them to stop, but she sensed they had reached this place many times before. In such a case, it was more important to understand the cause than to treat the symptom. "Are they always like this?"

Max nodded. "I'm actually surprised they made it halfway across the Atlantic before they lost it. And they wonder why I'd rather work on the holidays. Gio and Nick are like oil and water. Or gunpowder and a match. However you describe it, you don't want to stand between them. One day, one of them is going to snap."

"Were they always like that?" Julia asked, watching Gio take his laptop from one of his bags. *He's going to escape to where he is successful—work.*

Max shrugged. "I don't remember them fighting like this before our father died. Maybe they did, and I was too young to see it."

"How did your father die?"

"He was working in Venice. Don't ask me what an oil company CEO needs to do in a sinking city, but that's the story. A heart attack, I think. We don't talk about it. Gio brought him back to the U.S., buried him, took over the company, and has looked exactly that miserable ever since."

"Did Nick go with him?" Julia had to ask. She didn't want to picture Gio collecting his father's remains alone.

Max watched Gio walking back to sit with them and lowered his voice. "I don't know."

Gio returned to his seat and placed his computer on his lap, but he didn't open it. Julia reached over and took one of his hands in hers, giving it a supportive squeeze. He looked down at her, his eyes dark with suppressed emotions.

The more Julia learned about the man beside her, the more her heart opened to him. Although the four brothers were confined in a small aircraft together, the distance between them was clear. More than anything, she wished she knew how to reach past whatever had separated them.

She looked across at Max and said, "I'm an only child, but I always dreamed of having brothers or sisters. You're all lucky to have one another."

Gio's hand tightened on hers. "You can say that after what you witnessed a few minutes ago?"

Julia looked up at him with her heart in her eyes. "Being part of a family is a messy business, but it's worth it. A good friend of mine comes from a huge family, and the stories she tells would make your hair curl. Someone is always fighting with someone else. Sometimes the reasons are funny, other times sad. But when one of them is in need, they're there for each other. I imagine you and your brothers are the same."

"Gio, you really should have told her more about us. It's going to be depressing watching her lower her opinion of large families as she gets to know us." Max stood and walked away to join his brothers, who were sitting around a smaller table near the plane's galley.

In the quiet following Max's departure, Julia said, "Gio, your brothers..."

Gio broke contact with her and opened his laptop. "I don't want to discuss it," he said dismissively and started typing as if Julia no longer sat beside him.

The temptation to slam the laptop closed on his fingers was strong. She was itching to tell him how rude he was being, but there was a hint of something in his expression that made her hold her tongue. He wasn't trying to hurt her; he was hiding. The strong man beside her was lost when it came to overcoming whatever had happened to his family, and he dealt with it by withdrawing.

Julia slid her arm beneath his and hugged it. He looked up from his laptop with a scowl on his face. Still, Julia didn't let go. She held his eyes and continued to hug his arm to her. *You don't fool me, Gio. I know you're upset. I'm here if you need me.*

His expression softened. He leaned over and kissed her forehead, then seemed as surprised by his action as she was. He cleared his throat and said, "You should try to sleep. It'll be a long day if you don't."

She hid a smile and laid her head on his shoulder. She didn't know what the trip held for either of them, but in that moment, she was glad she'd agreed to go.

❧

The even rhythm of Julia's breath as she slept was calming. Gio placed his laptop on the floor beside him and closed his eyes. Nothing about Julia made sense. Every time she spoke he was reminded of how very different they were. At first, he'd thought he was drawn to her for purely sexual reasons. But having her curled up against him, supporting him even without fully understanding the situation, filled him with a warm feeling he couldn't deny.

Part of him wanted to push her away and list the reasons they didn't belong together. Part of him wanted to hold her close and tell her that nothing in his life had ever felt so right.

I don't want this.
Any of this.
Not her.
Not a weekend with relatives.
None of this.
Life is better when it's uncomplicated.
In control.

The exact opposite of how it had been for him since he'd met Julia.

He turned his head and looked down at her sleeping profile. His breath caught in his throat. *I shouldn't have brought her. I need a clear head to navigate the weekend.*

His three brothers returned to their seats across from him. Luke handed him a cup of steaming black coffee. He accepted it with a nod.

With Julia asleep at his side, he sipped his coffee and studied his brothers. Neither Nick nor Max would meet his eyes. Luke gave him a sympathetic smile.

What did Julia say about family? It's messy?
What are they waiting for me to say?
Whatever I say will be wrong.
It always is.

He glanced down at Julia again. *What would she do if our situations were reversed? She'd blurt out an apology. She wouldn't dress it up with excuses or worry about the possible backlash. She'd dive right in.*

Gio looked across at Nick and said, "I went too far earlier. What you do is your business."

Nick propped an ankle on top of his knee, leaned back, and asked nonchalantly, "Are you actually apologizing?"

Gio straightened, inadvertently waking Julia. She sat up, rubbed her eyes, and looked back and forth between them as if trying to remember where she was. She smiled up at Gio and—he couldn't help it—he smiled back.

Luke raised a hand to catch the attention of the flight attendant. "Julia, would you like a coffee?"

She shook her head. "Maybe a snack, though?"

Luke called the attendant over. Julia and all four brothers put in a request for a light fare of sandwiches and finger foods.

In the quiet after the attendant's departure, Julia asked, "How much longer until we arrive?"

Gio checked his watch. "Two hours at the most."

"Do you want to watch a movie?" Julia asked.

There was a unanimous shake of heads.

"Play a game?" she asked cheerfully.

Although Gio shook his head, Max leaned forward in his seat. "What kind of game?"

Luke pointed a thumb at his younger brother with a knowing smile. "Max is a professional gambler, so don't make it poker. We gave up trying to beat him back when all we had to lose was our allowance."

Julia's eyes rounded. "A professional gambler? What an interesting job."

Max shrugged. "It is. Everything in life is a gamble. For a while I lived solely off my poker winnings. However, now I build casinos around the world. So, Gio can finally admit to knowing me again."

Gio tensed at Max's comment. "Your profession never bothered me."

"Really?" Max asked, unconvinced.

Nick said in mock sympathy, "Don't feel bad, Max. He's ashamed of all of us."

Luke interjected, "Nick, can we make it to the island without another scene?"

Normally, Gio would have ended the conversation before it went further. He regularly told himself he didn't care what others thought, but this time he didn't lie to himself. "I'm proud of all of my brothers," Gio said, more harshly than he'd intended.

"Even me?" Nick pushed.

Gio answered without hesitation. "I may not agree with the choices you've made lately, Nick, but I understand why you make them."

Nothing in his life matched the rush of emotion he felt in response to Julia's light squeeze of his arm in approval.

Nick opened his mouth to say something, then closed it with a snap. Max looked like he wanted to say something more but decided against it.

Luke clapped his hands and said, "So, how about that game, Julia?"

She turned shyly to Gio. "It was a silly idea. We don't have to."

Although he usually viewed games as a waste of time, time was exactly what they had to fill, and he'd take anything that would distract from more excruciatingly awkward conversations. "We could use a game about now. What did you have in mind?"

Julia reached down into her bag and took out a small pile of index cards. "Rena thought I should know who I'm going to meet on the island. She made these index cards for me. One side has a name written on it. The other side has clues on how to recognize that person. We could see who is best at guessing the person from the description."

Cocking his head to the side, Luke asked, "Rena did that for you? Interesting."

Julia held the stack of cards to her chest for a moment. "She thinks I might be able to make a connection at the wedding."

Nick looked at Max and shrugged. "Okay, I'll bite. A connection for what?"

Julia instinctively brought a hand to her necklace, and she flashed a brave smile at Gio's three brothers. "I moved to New York to try to sell my jewelry designs. So far, nothing, but I'm not giving up. I'm hoping to find an investor."

Nick nodded toward Gio. "I'd say you've already met one."

Julia winked at Gio and said, "No, I'm just with him for the sex."

Max choked on the sip of coffee he'd just taken. Nick's mouth fell open, and Luke shook his head.

Gio's eyes flew to Julia's in surprise.

Julia burst into laughter. "You should see your faces. No wonder you fight so much. You're all way too serious." She composed herself, folded her hands in mock contriteness, and said with just a trace of humor, "Even my dad would have laughed at that joke."

Gio looked down at Julia, half coughed, then chuckled.

Julia's eyes were brimming with laughter, threatening to erupt again. She waved her hands in a plea for him to stop. "Don't laugh, Gio, because I shouldn't when I'm still trying to make a good impression."

"You have," Max said and joined in their laughter. "I didn't think anything could shock Nick, but I believe he's speechless."

Nick said, "I'm just trying to figure out how Gio ended up with a woman who is actually fun."

Julia smiled. "I may have scrambled his brains the first time I met him. I hit him with that lamp pretty hard."

Luke said, "I believe it was physicist Joseph Henry who said, Great discoveries only take root in minds well prepared to receive them. He needed some scrambling."

"Funny, Luke," Gio said gruffly, raising a hand to his temple as he remembered that blow. "It could have killed me."

Conversation was halted while the attendant set trays of food on a table between them. Once by themselves again, Max said, "I want to know why you hit him with a lamp."

Julia blushed. "I thought he was breaking into Rena's desk..." As she retold the story, Gio noticed his brothers were genuinely interested, and relaxing for the first time since they'd entered the plane. Julia had a gift when it came to breaking down barriers. As they joked together, Gio was reminded of how he and his brothers had interacted when they were younger.

Julia had given him a glimpse of the past, and he wasn't sure what to do with the way it made him feel.

The next two hours flew by. Conversation flowed easily, and Julia kept the mood light by periodically reading a new index card to the group. They took turns using the small bedroom in the back of the plane as a dressing room, slowly transforming from casual to party-ready.

When Julia returned to the main part of the plane dressed in a floor-length navy gown, Gio couldn't take his eyes off her. She'd styled her hair in a loose bun that made a man want to reach out and release those barely contained curls. The dress fit her snuggly and emphasized her curves so deliciously that had they been alone she wouldn't have kept it on for long.

She caught him looking at her, and the smile she gave him knocked what was left of his sanity out of him. In that instant, he didn't care about anything but having her again. By the way a blush spread up her cheeks, he knew she'd guessed his thoughts.

The pilot's voice interrupted and requested everyone fasten their seat belts for the final approach to Isola Santos.

Gio tensed instinctively as he was slammed back into reality. He looked out the side window and caught his first glimpse of the island. The enormous glass-and-chrome building Dominic Corisi had built still dominated a good fourth of the island. The sight of it made him angrier than he'd expected it to.

Julia was also looking out the window. She turned and asked, "That's the island? Wow, that is quite a compound. Did your family build that?"

"No," Gio said, hearing the disgust in his own voice. He leaned over her, and as the plane circled before landing, he pointed to a much smaller, stone mansion on the other side of the island. "That's the Andrade mansion."

Luke looked out the window beside him. "It's been in the family for hundreds of years."

Julia innocently continued on with a painful line of questioning. "So, what is the large glass compound? Are they leasing land to a university or something?"

Max looked at Gio cautiously. "Uncle Victor sold the island when he hit financial difficulties. The new owner built that glass shrine to himself."

"Mother offered to buy the island, but Dominic Corisi outbid us," Gio said bitterly.

"Your mother?" Julia asked, then looked as if she regretted saying it out loud.

"Surprised that we have one?"

"No," Julia said, wide-eyed. "Of course you have a mother. I'm sure she's very nice, too. She couldn't make it today?"

Max was the first to answer. "She never got along with our uncles. She came from old money and our father came from... let's just say... less-refined stock."

Nick defended his father's family. "The Andrades had money. Perhaps not at the Stanfield level, but enough that they summered on their private island each year. And this generation has more than made up for whatever they didn't have before."

Julia interjected, "So, we're not talking about the completely unacceptable type who would have to work year round. Thank God."

All four brothers turned to look at her. Julia merely raised her eyebrows and waited. Luke laughed and turned to Gio. "I do believe your girlfriend is just what this family needs."

Julia gave them each a cheeky smile that removed the sting from her words. "Just calling it like I see it."

Gio watched his brothers melt before her charm. *I keep telling myself what Julia and I have is nothing more than a physical attraction. She doesn't belong here. But what if I'm wrong?*

His stomach twisted painfully at the thought.

Blissfully unaware, Julia looked out the window again and said, "So, the new owner is letting your cousin get married on your old island. That's nice."

Max shook his head. "Stephan is marrying the sister of the man who bought the island. Corisi intends to return the island to Stephan as a wedding present. So, it looks like it's back in the family."

"Not *our* family," Gio said harshly. He regretted voicing those words as soon as they were out. In a heartbeat his brothers' expressions closed, and tension once again crackled in the air. Julia reached out and took his hand in hers.

The tires of the plane touched and bounced on the island runway.

After descending the stairs, he paused. Julia's eyes were round with wonder as she took in the manicured grounds, the visible security everywhere, and the party that was spilling out of the glass building and onto the lawn in front of it. In the middle of a group of adults, dressed in formal gowns and tuxedos, children chased each other, their laughter ringing out above the music of a live band.

The level of joy bubbling out of the house filled Gio with intense and conflicting emotions, holding him immobile even as his brothers began walking toward the house.

Julia tugged on his hand until he looked down at her again. She went up on her tiptoes and whispered, "What are you thinking?"

He studied the monstrosity of glass and chrome with disgust. "Only someone with a complete lack of appreciation for the beauty and history of the island would have built such an atrocity." He shared his thoughts aloud. "I want to throw a hundred rocks through those glass windows."

Julia made a funny grimace. "That wouldn't be my first choice of how to start the evening."

His breath came quicker as adrenaline rushed through his veins. He smiled down at her. "I'm angry. Furious, in fact. I haven't felt like this in years."

Julia's eyes widened again. "And that's a good thing?"

He tried to find the words to explain it but couldn't. "Yes, I believe it is." He'd held it in so long it had made him numb to everything else. Suddenly, he felt more alive than he had in years. Like he could finally breathe.

"Come on." Instead of heading toward the party, he led Julia toward a path leading to the other side of the island.

"Where are we going?" Julia asked as she lengthened her strides to keep up with him.

"There's something I want to show you."

The island was small enough that she didn't have to wonder about their destination for long. A ten-minute brisk walk brought them to the steps of the building he thought he'd never see again. "This was my father's house."

"Is it locked?" she asked.

He lifted a pulled a loose stone from the foundation of the house, took out a key, and said, "Not for long."

"Are you sure we can go inside?"

He spared her a quick look before swinging the door open. The home's classic Mediterranean style gave it a timeless quality. Its white walls, accented with intricate tile work, could easily have been the result of a renovation, but they were original to the home.

Gio led Julia down the hall, into what had once been the study. What little furniture remained in the room was covered with white cloths, making the room seem abandoned and oddly preserved at the same time. He stood there, feeling as if he had one foot in the present and one in the past. "I always thought this house would one day belong to me. It has been passed down from the oldest son to the oldest son for generations." He walked over to the mantel of a large fireplace and ran his hand across the dusty marble. "When my father died and it didn't come to me, I was furious. The sale of it was a final slap in the face." He walked to a bookcase and took down a book that had been left behind. "I was twenty-five. I'd been struggling for a year to fill my father's shoes at Cogent. I didn't confront my uncles. Instead, I put all my energy into what I could change, and that was the profitability of my family's company." He turned to Julia and said, "I should have fought for this place. I should have made it mine."

Their eyes met and Julia's heart thudded in her chest. She shook her head. He was finally opening up to her. She wanted to tell him how much it meant to her, but she knew he needed to be left uninterrupted.

He left her side to search the remaining items on the surrounding shelves. He ran a hand over the molding.

"What are you looking for?" Julia couldn't contain her curiosity.

"Something that probably isn't here," Gio said as he continued pulling old books from the shelves and flipping through them.

"What?"

He walked to where a desk had once been and looked around the room. "The truth."

Julia followed Gio out of the library and into each of the downstairs rooms. Not much had been left behind. Every item of value must have been removed before the sale.

Gio flipped a switch in one of the closets, but the area remained dark. Not that there was anything inside to be illuminated. Speaking more to himself than to her, Gio said, "The two houses must run on separate generators." He ran his hand along the intricate wood paneling, absently caressing the house. "I remember reading an interview with Corisi after he bought the island. He planned to knock this house down. He considered it old ruins."

Gio walked back into the main hall, and Julia followed him. She knew Gio was far away in his thoughts, and that was okay with her. *What did he mean when he said he was looking for the truth?*

They walked up one side of a double curved stairway that led off the foyer. At the top, Julia let herself imagine filling the space below with people and laughter. "This must have been an incredible place to entertain."

"It has ten bedrooms. When I was a child, they were always full. My father said it was the same when he was young. Andrades have been born here. Some have even died here. My grandfather passed away in his sleep right here in the house, surrounded by his family."

"I can see why you wouldn't want it to be knocked down." Julia could only imagine Gio's bond to the house. The home and factory she was fighting for had only been in their family for one generation. To lose something that was so linked to your family's history must have been devastating. "Did your mother also love this place?" It was hard for Julia to imagine her letting it go if she had.

"My mother refused to step inside it."

Interesting.

Gio walked ahead of her into one of the rooms. She lingered in the upper hallway, running her hand along the areas where slightly darker patches of wallpaper revealed where paintings had once hung. *Family paintings? Famous Italian artists? What would they have displayed?*

What could anyone hate about this beautiful house?

Was it because Gio's grandfather died here?

Julia turned from the wall, realizing she had no idea where Gio had gone. She hugged herself as a sudden chill went up her back.

It would take more than that to keep me away.

Ghosts aren't real.

I mean, not the ones that move things around and scare people.

Her father would have argued that the universe was full of an infinite number of things the human mind could not comprehend. Julia smiled as she remembered her mother's rebuttal to that theory. "Show me the proof. Things fall. Lights flicker. To me, that's not evidence of a ghost. Is every spirit a klutz that can only make a mess? You want me to believe in one? Show me a ghost that washes dishes or folds my laundry. Then I'll believe."

She has a point, Grandpa Andrade. If you're here, do something useful and help Gio find whatever it is he's looking for.

Julia's cell phone rang in her purse and she screamed. She scrambled to take it out, dropped it, picked it back up, then screamed again when it rang in her hands.

I am such an idiot.

Caller ID showed a blocked number.

She hesitated, then laughed again as it continued to ring. *What do I think, this is a call from the other side? More likely it's a telemarketer trying to sell me a place in Italy because some cookie I downloaded is announcing my location.*

Julia gave herself a mental shake and answered her phone. "Hello?"

"I'm disappointed in you, Julia."

Another chill went down Julia's back. *Worse than a specter...* "Mrs. Andrade, what a... surprise... to hear from you."

Her hand went protectively to her throat. Although she had done nothing wrong, Julia spun to make sure she was still alone and almost screamed again when she saw Gio standing just behind her. She covered her mouth with one hand.

Mountain climbers shouldn't be afraid of heights.

And women who run halfway around the world with men they recently met shouldn't be so jumpy. *Be calm. Sophisticated. I've got this.*

He nodded toward the phone and mouthed, "Who is that?"

Julia froze. *Say something. Don't just stare at him.* Her mind raced for a lie or an explanation, but none came. She held the phone out awkwardly, completely at a loss for what to say.

Gio took it and pressed the speakerphone button.

No.

"Are you alone?" his mother asked.

Gio's eyes narrowed as he recognized his mother's voice. He looked to Julia for an explanation, but all she could do was shrug. *This isn't good. His mother already doesn't like me. I'm pretty sure this won't help.* She made a grab for her phone, but

Gio held it just out of her reach. She pleaded with her eyes for him to give her the phone, but he nodded for her to answer his mother.

"Are you daft, girl? It's an easy yes or no question."

Gio held her eyes, willing her to do the unthinkable. *This isn't right. But what she said to me back in New York wasn't right, either. Maybe he has the right to know what his mother is up to.* "Yes, I'm alone."

In a cutting tone she said, "I tried to be nice to you, Julia. You should have taken my offer. A smart girl would have. Now you'll come back to nothing. After I tell Gio about you, he won't give you the time of day."

A deep frown settled over Gio's expression. His eyes were cold and unreadable. Barely above a whisper, Julia said, "There's nothing to tell."

"The truth is what I say it is. He won't believe you over me."

A deep fury contorted Gio's features. "I wouldn't be so sure of that, Mother."

"Gio." Her voice jumped an octave as she said his name. Then it quickly became conciliatory. "I'm trying to protect you, that's all. It's obvious this girl is only after our money."

"What's obvious is that I can no longer believe anything you tell me," Gio said coldly and hung up.

Julia hugged her stomach. Although a small part of her felt his mother had earned whatever grief her actions had brought her, the scene she'd just witnessed broke her heart. Her love for her own mother, and her sadness as the woman who had raised her so well slipped away, made her want to shake both of them. *Call her back. Tell her you love her. Give her a chance to apologize.*

Gio stared down at the phone. His hand tightened on it until the case cracked from the pressure. He threw the broken phone over the banister in disgust.

"Oh," Julia exclaimed involuntarily as she grabbed for it.

He looked back at her.

Julia watched the phone bounce once, then shatter on the floor below. *I did tell him that throwing things was a good way to express anger. I just didn't know he'd start with my stuff.* "It's fine. I mean, who would I need to call anyway, right?"

"I'll get you another phone."

Julia looked over her shoulder at him. "It's not a big deal."

"I said I'd replace it."

"Do what you want to do. That's what you do anyway."

"Are we actually arguing about your damn phone?"

Julia clung to the railing with both hands. Watching him fight with his mother had made her angry. And feel as helpless as she felt each time she spoke with her own mother. But Gio's mother wasn't sick. They didn't have to do this to each other. They still had time, if they chose to work things out. "Yes, because it didn't have to happen like this. You should have given the phone back to me when I asked for it."

"And when she came to me with lies about you? What then?"

"Maybe she wouldn't have." When Gio looked at her doubtfully, Julia threw her hands up in the air. "I don't have all the answers, but I do know that life is short and cruel. If you love her at all, figure out why she's angry. Appreciate that you have something not everyone does—time to fix things. Do you know what I'd give to have my mother fully back with me for even one day? I'd give anything to sit down with her and know she knew me. And not because my father told her who I was, but because she actually remembered me and our lives together." Julia stopped and wiped a tear from her cheek. She hadn't intended to say any of that. "I'm sorry."

He pulled her to him and simply hugged her. "Don't be." He rested his chin on her forehead. After a moment he asked, "What did she mean when she said you should have accepted her offer?"

"Does it matter?" she hedged.

"Yes."

"Why? The details won't change what you know."

"Julia." He said her name in a tone that meant he wasn't giving up until she told him everything.

Julia closed her eyes and said, "She offered me two hundred thousand dollars if I went back to Rhode Island instead of coming to the wedding with you."

He held her back from him and searched her face. "The exact amount you need to save your father's business."

"Yes," Julia said hoarsely. There was a look in his eyes she'd seen before. It filled her with a warmth she fought against.

Don't start imagining he's falling in love.

Don't do that to yourself.

"But you didn't take it," he said softly.

Her breath caught in her throat. "I promised I'd come here with you."

With a groan, he lowered his mouth to hers. He kissed the curve of her neck. He raised his head, his eyes full of desire. For a moment she thought he was going to say something, then his mouth descended on hers, claiming it with an intensity that had her sagging against him with pleasure. His tongue was hot and demanding, encircling hers possessively. His hands sought the zipper of her gown. Their kiss paused just long enough for him to undo it. He held the dress as she stepped out of it, then dropped it over the banister.

He impatiently slid her underwear off and sent them floating down to the foyer below. His mouth was caressing her everywhere: her neck, her shoulders, tickling behind her ear. He lifted her, naked, and balanced her on the banister.

She clutched at his shoulders, out of passion and also a twinge of fear. Until now, she would have said that the most daring place she'd ever had sex was on a secluded beach. Danger heightened the intensity of the experience. She unbuttoned the front of his shirt, desperate to feel more of him.

There was something about being held by him, trusting him to protect her, meeting him in this very physical sense, that brought their lovemaking to an entirely new level. She gave herself to him in that moment. Completely. And she knew she would never want or trust another man as much as she did Gio.

With one arm supporting her back, he slid a hand up her thigh. She shuddered in anticipation. He gently caressed the inside of each of her thighs. Teasing her. She wanted to feel his fingers on her, in her. Helpless before him, dripping wet with need, she whimpered.

He raised his head and looked down into her eyes. "Do you know what you do to me?"

She closed her eyes and shook her head, unable to speak.

"It has never been like this with anyone else."

His hand slid over the outside of her wet folds. One finger slid between them and began to rub her clit with a rhythm that had her writhing against him, no longer caring about the floor far below. All that mattered was his touch and how it made her feel.

"Say you're mine, Julia. Tell me nothing else matters. It's just you and me and this."

He thrust a finger deep inside her and she cried out with pleasure. In that moment, she almost said she loved him, but she knew that wasn't what he wanted to hear. He was taking possession of her body on the most primal level, and he wanted to know she gave it to him willingly.

"I'm yours, Gio."

He lifted her and she wrapped her legs around his waist. With his hands on her waist, he turned and took a few long strides until she felt a solid wall against her back. He unbuckled his belt and opened the front of his trousers, then braced her against the wall as he deftly opened a foil wrapper and sheathed himself. His tip teased at the opening of her wet center.

He kissed her deeply while he thrust inside her. She gasped into his mouth. This was no controlled lovemaking. His hands bit into her waist as he held her and pounded again and again. There was pleasure and pain—mixing and building within her with this wild mating. She spread her legs wider for him.

As she spiraled toward an orgasm.

Heat spread through her. She was beyond the ability to speak.

He shuddered against her as he came inside her. They held each other, breathing raggedly. Still inside her, he groaned. "I can't get enough of you."

"Is that a bad thing?" Julia asked. *Because I feel the same.*

He slid her slowly to the ground and stepped back. "It is when I know how wrong I am for you."

They both froze at the sound of the front door opening below. A female voice asked, "Do you think they're inside?" *Maddy.*

Julia looked into Gio's eyes and held back a nervous giggle. He adjusted his pants, picked his shirt off the floor, and offered it to her. She slipped it on, grateful that it hung down almost to her knees.

A male voice answered her. "I doubt it. Gio swore he'd never return here." *Luke.*

"People can change. You didn't think he'd ever accept the invitation."

"I was wrong. Looks like I'm wrong again. He's here."

"Why do you say that?"

"Because those are Julia's clothes."

Julia covered her mouth to stop the audible gasp that escaped her. She took a step back against the wall.

"Oh," Maddy said. Then said again, with more emphasis, "*Oh.*"

Julia covered her face with her hands in mortification. Gio pulled her back into his arms and kissed her forehead.

In a louder voice, Maddy said, "If you two can hear me, I'm really glad you came. We're going back now, but I was worried when you didn't come in with the others. I wanted to make sure you were okay." She laughed. "It looks like you are. So, come on over to the rehearsal dinner when you're ready."

Luke said, "Julia, have I mentioned how good you are for my brother? Don't let him scare you off."

Julia held her breath until she heard the door close behind them, Then joked, "Well, I've hit a new level of embarrassment."

Gio looked angry again, and Julia was sorry she'd spoken aloud. She laid one of her hands softly on one of his cheeks. "I don't care what they think of me, Gio."

Face tight, eyes burning with an emotion she couldn't decipher, he growled, "I do. You deserve better than this. Better than me."

She smiled up at him, wishing she knew what to say to remove some of the sadness in his tone. "I don't know about that, but I do deserve some of the hors d'oeuvres I saw them serving. I'm starving."

"After everything, you still want to go?"

She searched his eyes for a moment. "I don't care about the party. Or the wedding. I care about you. We can leave now if you want, or we can go in there and meet every last damn relative you have. What do you want to do?"

He hugged her to him. "What the hell is someone as nice as you doing with a man like me?"

"You're not nearly as awful as you think you are, Gio."

He shook his head and took her hand, leading her down the stairs toward her clothing. "You don't know me."

She stopped halfway down the stairs. He turned two stairs below her, which brought them eye to eye. "But I want to."

He nodded and started leading her across the foyer toward the door.

Julia, still clad only in his shirt, pulled him to a stop. "I should probably get my dress first."

He looked down at her and a lusty smile spread across his face. "And I'll need my shirt back."

She laughed up at him. "We're already late."

He kissed the line of her jaw and whispered in her ear, "Then it won't matter, will it?"

Chapter Eighteen

THE SUN WAS dipping over the horizon the second time Gio and Julia approached the large glass mansion. This time Gio didn't hesitate. Holding Julia's hand, he walked straight across the lawn, up the stairs, and through the large glass doors. An older man crossed to meet them as soon as they entered.

"Gio, it's good to see you again."

Gio didn't return the compliment. He merely nodded and said, "Julia, this is my uncle, Alessandro."

His uncle smiled warmly and winked at her. "The Andrades have always had good taste in women." He looked over his shoulder and waved for his wife to join them. "My own wife is as beautiful today as she was the day I met her. Elise, come meet Gio's date. Imagine the babies these two would make."

Elise rushed forward and swatted at her husband. "Don't mind him. Ever since Maddy gave us a grandchild he has baby on the brain." She gave Julia a kiss of welcome on both cheeks.

Looking playfully affronted, Alessandro covered his wounded heart with one hand. "Theirs would not be any baby. With my brother gone, Gio is like a son to me. His children would be my grandchildren as much as mine are."

Julia felt Gio tense beside her and she quickly intervened. "I noticed there is quite a large group here already. Are they all staying in the main house?"

Alessandro looked puzzled by her question, then answered, "Oh, yes, there are plenty of rooms. Or were you asking about the mansion? We didn't open it for this event. It's empty anyway. I don't know if the generator would work after all this time. I'd have to ask Dominic if anyone has maintained it since he's owned it. Honestly, I don't have the heart to go see it.

Perhaps after Stephan renovates it I will feel differently. It will be nice to have it back in the family."

Gio's hand tightened painfully on Julia's arm. Julia glanced up and cringed at the burning fury she saw in his eyes. Alessandro saw it, too, and a line of concern formed on his forehead.

Elise's light tone revealed that she had missed the building tension. "I looked for both of you when your brothers arrived, but they said you went for a walk. I can understand wanting to after such a long flight. We're so happy to have you here. Come, let me introduce you to some of your cousins who were not able to make it to New York this summer."

Julia whispered as they walked. "You're hurting my arm, Gio."

He looked down and instantly released her. "Sorry. I wasn't aware..."

She took his hand in hers and gave it a supportive squeeze. "I know." His features were set in harsh lines.

As she and Gio followed Alessandro, Julia felt like she'd stepped into a movie. The men were handsomely attired in tuxedos that screamed of money and power. The women were dressed in floor-length gowns and dripping with diamonds. Julia fingered the prototype necklace she'd worn. The metal was copper instead of gold. The stones were faux.

Did I really think I could network here? Which one of these women would spare a second look at my costume jewelry when they're wearing enough diamonds to buy and sell a small country?

Julia recognized Nicole from across the room. She was exquisitely dressed in a flowing powder-blue Prada gown and looked perfectly at home amidst the somewhat gaudy display of wealth. After Rena's informative crash course in the wedding guests, Julia understood why. Nicole had been raised in this world, and her brother was one of the top ten wealthiest men in the world.

Nicole caught Julia watching her and said something to the tall blond man beside her. The man, who had to be Stephan Andrade, looked up and nodded to his fiancée, and they both started walking across the large foyer toward them.

Alessandro hugged Nicole to his side and turned to introduce her to Julia. "Nicole, have you met Gio's girlfriend?"

If possible, Nicole's smile grew wider at the label. She leaned in and kissed Julia's cheeks in greeting. "Yes, I have. Welcome, Julia. I'm so pleased you could make it."

Stephan shook Gio's hand. "Thank you for coming."

"You can thank Madison. She was... persuasive," Gio said with some irony.

Stephan laughed. "That's being kind. Maddy is too used to getting her way. She means well, though. And it's impossible for any of us to stay upset with her, so I suppose it's our fault she has boundary issues." More seriously, he added, "Whatever brought you, it means a lot to me that you came. Nothing is more important than family."

Alessandro smacked Gio on the shoulder. "It's good to have all of us together again."

Gio made a sound deep in his chest, and Julia tugged on his hand. He looked down at her, and she did her best to send him a telepathic message. *Behave. They love you.* Julia turned her attention to Nicole and said, "You must be out-of-your-mind excited. What a beautiful location for a wedding. I saw tents going up on the far lawn. Is that where the ceremony will be?"

Nicole said, "That's where the reception will be. For the ceremony, we're doing something outside." She smiled dreamily up at her fiancé. "There is a hill about halfway between this house and the old Andrade mansion. At the very top of it, you can see both clearly. There isn't room for chairs at the top, but the symbolism of two families coming together through our union is worth having everyone stand for the short time we'll be there." She looked across at Julia shyly. "That probably sounds corny."

Julia shook her head. "Not at all. It's a beautiful idea."

Innocently, Nicole said, "You and Gio should take a walk over tomorrow and see the old house. It's lovely."

"It really is," Julia agreed spontaneously, then blushed. *I did not mean to say that.*

Stephan looked at Gio curiously. "You went over to see the old place? I didn't realize you had any interest in it."

Face tight, Gio said, "It was part of my childhood as much as yours."

Stephan nodded slowly, then glanced at his uncle with a curious expression. Alessandro shook his head tersely in a move that clearly meant, Drop the subject.

Nicole gave the room a quick scan. "I have to tell Maddy you're here, Julia. I wonder where she went."

"She knows," Julia said, then covered her traitorous mouth with one hand. *Thank God I'm not a spy. I'd fail miserably at it.*

Nicole's eyebrows shot up in surprise. "Really? She didn't say anything. That little stinker. Usually she tells me everything."

Hopefully not everything. Julia bit her lip beneath her hand.

"There's Abby," Nicole exclaimed with excitement and waved her over.

A beautiful brunette walked over with a tall dark-haired man. The crowd parted for them in a way they hadn't even for the bride- and groom-to-be. Abby and Dominic Corisi: the new American royal family. Even Julia found them easy to recognize. Their whirlwind romance and wedding had been highly publicized, and their new daughter was on the cover of every gossip magazine at the grocery store. The billionaire, and the middle-school teacher who had won his heart. What was not to love about their story?

Starstruck, Julia watched the beautiful couple and sighed audibly.

Dominic greeted Gio with a handshake. "Good to see you again."

Abby shook Gio's hand warmly, then looked from Julia to Nicole.

A mischievous smile spread across Nicole's face as she pointed at Julia. "This is *Julia*. She came with Gio."

Abby's face brightened with unexpected recognition. "*The* Julia?"

Gio tensed beside Julia. "Excuse me?"

Dominic hugged his wife to his side and said with some humor, "You don't want to know."

Suddenly not looking very happy, Gio looked down at Julia suspiciously.

Abby noticed and blushed. "Wow, I have been hanging out with my sister too much."

Stephan looked back and forth between the two. "Is this about the bet?"

Nicole glared up at him and said, "No." He looked about to say something else, but Nicole quickly said, "Don't ruin it."

Alessandro let out a hearty laugh. "Gio, now that you're back you'll have to get used to the women plotting against us. Don't worry about it. It's always harmless. And if you ask Maddy, she'll tell you everything. She's the weak link."

Nicole whispered something to Abby.

Julia joked to Alessandro, "That may change after those two talk to her."

The older man bent his tall frame and gave Julia the saddest puppy-dog expression she'd ever seen on a grown man. "Could you resist your father if he looked at you like this?" Alessandro turned his head more to the side, focused his eyes on the floor then, slowly raised them to meet Julia's, silently pleading.

Julia burst out laughing. "You've got me. I would tell you everything."

Straightening and puffing with pride, Alessandro rewarded Julia with a pleased smile. "It's all in the eyes."

Nicole chastised him playfully. "Uncle Alessandro. You're shameless."

He shrugged, clearly not bothered by her teasing. He waved to someone across the room and said, "If you'll all excuse me. I was going to introduce Gio and Julia around, but it looks like that's not necessary." Before he walked away he said, "It is good to have you here, Gio."

A woman came by and motioned for Nicole to follow her. Nicole said, "The photographer would like to take pictures of the wedding party now." She smiled at Julia. "We'll talk later."

Stephan nodded to Gio and followed Nicole into one of the side rooms. Abby and Dominic excused themselves and did the same.

Gio took Julia by the arm and guided her in the opposite direction. "I didn't realize I had brought *the* Julia to the wedding. Do you know what they meant?"

Not one to lie, Julia answered honestly. "Not entirely. I think the women are hoping that you'll settle down, get married, and become close to this side of the family again."

"What does that have to do with you?"

Julia took a deep breath. *I'm sure he didn't mean that the way it sounded. Still, let's see if this takes some wind out of his sail.* "They seem to think the right woman can bring a man back from even the darkest place."

Instead of countering her comment or brushing it off, Gio mulled it for a moment before saying, "And what do you think?"

Mouth dry, Julia said, "I suppose it depends on the man and if he wants to come back."

He pulled her into a secluded corner, his eyes dark with emotion. "People don't change."

Julia put a hand on his chest, just above his heart. "What a sad world it would be if that were true."

He kissed her forehead. "You are one amazing woman, Julia. I wish..."

She covered his mouth with her hand. "Sometimes less is more. I am happy with amazing."

⚃

As Gio guided Julia through the party, it was easy to forget why he'd come. A constant stream of family members came over to greet them. Many of them he'd lost touch with. Some he was meeting for the first time. Although his father was one of three sons, the generation before theirs had been larger. First, second, third generation—the level of separation wasn't mentioned. About half the people in the room called themselves his cousin.

Random children he didn't recognize ran up and down the stairs in what appeared to be an organized game of hide-and-seek. Some parents gave chase; some gave up.

After the formal speeches of thanks by Nicole and Stephan, Victor Andrade stood at the top of a wide stairway with a microphone in his hand. The crowd quieted again.

"There is no greater gift than to be able to share the end of my son's bachelorhood with all of our friends and family. We welcome Nicole into our family and look forward to the little ones they will bring to us. For now, let's enjoy the ones we have." He beckoned to someone off to one side. His blonde wife stepped forward, leading several men carrying large white polished boards. "Katrine saw this in a magazine and fell in love with the idea."

The crowd watched as the workers quickly transformed one side of the stairway into a wide slide with a thick white pad at the bottom of it. One of the men handed Victor and his wife what looked like a white, velvet mattress with handles sewn into the top. They sat side by side at the top of the stairs. Victor said, "After the children have their fill, I hope you will try this for yourselves. Life is too short not to fill it with as much love and laughter as you can squeeze into it."

They pushed off from the top, and the crowd cheered as they flew down the slide and came to a gentle stop on the padded bottom. Laughing, Victor stood, then offered a hand to his wife and helped her up. She fixed her hair with one hand and beamed a smile at the surrounding crowd.

A herd of children charged up the other stairway and formed a line.

This was what his mother had always loathed about her husband's family. He remembered as a child being told to sit instead of join in. A Stanfield would never laugh as loudly they did. A Stanfield always remembered the importance of the family's reputation.

She'd done her best to keep his brothers and him separate from what she considered vulgar behavior. Yes, he had visited the island many times, but he'd never stayed overnight. Every visit had felt like a betrayal to his mother, who said they had never accepted her as one of them.

Nor, she'd warned, would they ever accept her sons.

He'd believed her.

He'd believed everything. He hated that he was no longer sure he should have.

Gio felt his gut twist with guilt. His brothers were off to one side of the room, included but still separate. Despite their earlier acceptance of the invitation to come, he knew they also had mixed feelings. Their mother stood between them and exuberance as surely as if she were there chastising them for being tempted to join in.

At his side, Julia pulled on his hand and asked, "Do you want to try it?"

He shook his head, not knowing what she was referring to.

"The slide," she clarified and looked at it with longing. "Have you ever seen anything so incredible?"

His answer stuck in his throat as he took in her unfiltered excitement. "No," he answered honestly. His heart beat double-time in his chest. Julia didn't cling to everything she'd ever done wrong and let it hold her back. She was more alive in that moment than he'd ever allowed himself to be, and it made him want to experience the wedding through her eyes.

A teasing grin lit her face as she said, "I dare you to do it with me."

"I don't accept dares," he said decisively.

"You should," she went up on her tiptoes and whispered in his ear. "They can be fun."

Her voice sent shivers of pleasure down his spine and he was instantly, painfully hard. "There are many things I want to do with you. Trying out that slide is not one of them."

"I suppose that officially makes me more daring than you," Julia said with a yawn.

He frowned down at her. "Really?"

She studied her nails. "Sure. I flew off to a foreign country with you. That's brave. You are afraid to look foolish in front of your own family. Not so brave."

He took her by the arm, half amused, half insulted by her assessment of him. "Well, we can't have that, can we?"

She hopped with excitement beside him. They'd almost made it to the stairs when his three brothers intercepted them.

Max blocked their way. "Hang on. Are you actually going up there?"

Nick raised a doubtful eyebrow. "Planning to dismantle it?"

Gio stepped around his brothers and continued to guide Julia toward the stairs.

Max asked, "Has he lost his mind?"

"No," Luke said, "his heart."

Gio stumbled as his brother's words slammed into him.

A quick glance down at Julia made Gio groan.

She smiled up at him. A big, happy smile revealed she'd heard Luke.

He should tell her Luke was wrong. He was not falling in love with her.

But he'd never liked to lie.

Chapter Nineteen

JULIA WAS WALKING back from the powder room when a smiling pregnant woman who didn't waste time with small talk hijacked her with a warm hug. "Maddy."

Maddy didn't let go as she said, "Luke was telling me how good he thinks you are for Gio. I thought the same thing when I first met you, but when you went sliding down the stairs together—I saw Gio laugh. I love you."

Okay, this is awkward. Julia gave her back a quick pat and coughed. "You're choking me."

With a light, embarrassed chuckle, Maddy released her. "I'm sorry. My emotions are all over the place. I'm just happy for you and Gio." A big smile spread across her face. "And a little envious. I remember what it was like to not be able to keep my hands off Richard. It's still good, but children make it more difficult to sneak off together."

Julia coughed again, and her face warmed with a blush. "Could we forget about earlier?" A sudden thought came to her as she remembered what Alessandro had said about his daughter. "You didn't tell anyone, did you?"

It was Maddy's turn to blush. "No one who would say anything. Don't worry."

Julia covered her eyes with one hand. Every floor should have an escape option. You click your heels twice and it swallows the mortified up, depositing them... where didn't matter... as long as it was far away.

In a moment of self-awareness, Maddy put a sympathetic hand on Julia's shoulder and said, "I know my family is a bit much to get used to, but we don't get involved unless we care."

Julia lowered her hand. "No, I'm sorry. My head is still spinning from all of this. Sometimes it feels like I've walked into a dream—a magical, beautiful world. Then I remind myself that dreams are something you wake up from." She met Maddy's eyes seriously. "I don't want to wake up."

Maddy hugged her again, but this time quickly. "Maybe you won't have to. Come on, there are a few more people I'd like to introduce you to before you go back to your date." After taking two steps, she stopped again and said, "Speaking of you and Gio, my father doesn't approve of you sharing a room. I tried to explain to him that you're in the stage of your relationship where really it would be best for everyone if you have one, but he's old-fashioned."

Julia's eyebrows rose. "You talked to him about me? About Gio? About me and Gio?"

Maddy started walking again in a rush. "I couldn't help it. He gave me that sad look and I cracked. It's some kind of parental mind control."

Julia kept pace with Maddy, but she was thinking back to her earlier conversation with Alessandro and wondered if he'd known then. "I can't believe you told your father."

"He won't say anything. Don't worry. He likes you."

❧

Alessandro closed the door of the ultramodern bookless library he'd invited Gio into.

He waved for Gio to come farther inside. "It's good to see you smiling."

For just a moment, Gio clung to the uncomplicated happiness he'd found with Julia within the chaotic Andrade celebration. He'd always thought of himself as a man who had no patience for children. However, when he'd reached the bottom of the slide the first time he'd found himself eye level with a clapping little girl dressed in a frock that made her look like a doll. "You're fast!"

"Higher mass objects have higher force on an incline plane," he had explained as he stood up.

Julia had taken the hand he offered her and bent down to explain to the girl, "We're bigger than you, so we go faster."

"Would I go fast if I went with you?"

Gio had looked around for the girl's mother. "Oh, I don't think that would be a good..."

"I bet you would," Julia had said as if he hadn't spoken, and offered her other hand to the little girl. "Let's try it. My name is Julia."

Big brown eyes had studied both of them. Then she'd taken Julia's hand. "I'm Anna. I'm one of the flower girls tomorrow. I get a basket and roses and a big pink dress. I picked the dress myself because I'm all grown up now. I pick my own clothes. I can't tie shoes yet, but we use Velcro. My brother knows how to tie shoes. He's eight. But he isn't a flower girl. He's a boy. And he doesn't get a dress because boys don't wear dresses. My dress is pink. Nicole said I could pick whatever color I wanted because I'm important in the wedding. I carry the flowers. And I picked pink because princesses wear pink." She'd stopped halfway up the stairs and directed a question to Gio. "Do you like this dress? It's pink, too."

She'd spun in front of him in her satin dress and stumbled, falling down a stair. Gio had caught the girl and steadied her. He hadn't realized he was scowling down at her until she touched the middle of her forehead and said, "You shouldn't frown like that. It gives you a wrinkle right here. And you're old. Wrinkles stay on old people. Are you my cousin Gio?"

Gio had opened his mouth to answer, but the little girl was already speaking again. "My mom told me to stay out of his way. She said he can be grumpy, but you're not grumpy, so you can't be him." She'd spun and started up the stairs again. "Come on, slowpokes. Mom said I can go down the slide five times. Does this count? I'm sharing it with you. I don't think it counts. She told me five times and then I have to go upstairs to bed. So, tell her it doesn't count. I don't want to go to bed yet. This party is fun. Isn't it fun?"

When the little girl sprinted ahead, Gio had growled into Julia's ear, "She was cute before she started talking."

Julia had joked, "She's not so bad. She's just excited. Come on—smile. You don't want to give yourself a wrinkle. I hear they stay on old people."

"Old, huh? You'll pay for that tonight."

After stealing a quick kiss, Julia had laughed and sprinted up the stairs, saying, "I certainly hope so."

The memory of the entire exchange brought an involuntary smile to Gio's face.

Alessandro cleared his throat loudly, bringing Gio back to the present. "Have you been drinking, Gio?"

"No," he said curtly, but he could understand the question. He wasn't acting like himself. He didn't feel like himself. For once, he felt like the past didn't need to have a stranglehold on him. He could make amends. He could be free.

Alessandro took a seat on one of the couches. "Please, sit."

Gio shook his head and remained standing. "I'd rather stand. What did you need to talk to me about?"

"You know we're happy to have you here, Gio."

Never one who had been open with his emotions, Gio merely pocketed his hands and waited. He doubted Alessandro had pulled him aside simply to express that sentiment.

His uncle walked over to the window and said, "Tomorrow Dominic Corisi will present the Isola Santos deed to Stephan and Nicole. Will that be a problem?"

There it was. The reason for their meeting.

Gio straightened to his full height. "What are you asking?"

"I always thought you weren't interested in the island or the old house." When Gio said nothing, Alessandro pushed. "But you were, weren't you?"

"I would not have offered to purchase it had I not been," Gio bit out.

"Purchase? Your mother returned the deed to me. It was in your father's possession. Why would you offer to buy something that was already yours?"

Just as his mother had predicted, his uncle wanted to turn him against her. "My mother said she never had the deed."

Alessandro pinched the bridge of his nose. "She lied. She returned it to us a few weeks after your father died. She said you had all discussed it and decided that owning it would bring back too many bad memories. I believed her. Especially considering the circumstances of your father's death."

Confusion and anger swirled within Gio.

Someone had lied.

He didn't yet know who.

"I see." But he didn't. Nothing made sense to him anymore. He had next to no connection to his uncle anymore. Why this intricate cover-up story?

Alessandro appeared genuinely distressed. "We never would have sold the island if we had known you wanted it."

Uncovering one lie only revealed more. "You expect me to believe that?"

Affronted, Alessandro rose to his full height and said, "You're family, for God's sake."

Family. He was beginning to hate that term. "That label doesn't mean as much to me as it once did."

Alessandro reached out as if he were going to put a hand on Gio's shoulder in support, then let his hand drop to his side.

He'd come for answers, but he was leaving with more questions. If his uncles were as cold and conniving as he'd been raised to believe they were, why were they making such a production out of pretending to care about him now?

Was this why the invitation scared his mother? She'd even gone so far as trying to pay off Julia—why? *Did she think it would stop him from coming here?*

"I should have spoken directly to you and your brothers. Patrice asked us not to talk to you about it. She said it was too upsetting for you."

Gio spun on his heel and walked to the door, then stopped and, without turning, asked, "Alessandro, did you know about my father? About Venice?"

"Yes."

"Didn't you think we deserved to know?"

"It was not my place to say anything."

Gio nodded once, a cold fury filling him.

Behind him, his uncle called out, "Gio, where are you going?"

With his hand on the door handle, Gio spoke without turning. "There is nothing here for me now."

His uncle spoke softly. "What would you have me do?"

"What you have always done for me—nothing." Gio walked out the door and closed it firmly behind him.

Chapter Twenty

JULIA'S HEAD WAS still spinning with the names of everyone Maddy had introduced her to. She doubted she'd ever been hugged as much in her life as she had that night. The experience had certainly changed her opinion of the rich and famous. At least these rich and these famous. She'd expected to feel out of place, but the Andrade clan knew how to make a guest feel welcome. Although they dressed in more expensive clothing than her friends at home, they were just as quick to play pranks or tease one other with an embarrassing recollection.

This is going to be an amazing weekend.

"Come on," Gio said harshly and took Julia by the arm.

"What?" Julia asked in surprise as she tried to keep up with his long strides—not an easy feat in heels. "What happened?"

He didn't answer until they had cleared the front door and were walking down the path. "We're leaving."

Julia dug in her heels and halted them both abruptly. "Whoa. An hour ago you were happy and mingling. What did I miss?"

"Nothing."

She looked down at her arm. "Really? Because you're dragging me around like something happened."

He released her and frowned. He let out a long sigh. "I need to get out of here."

"Apparently."

"Let's go." He took her arm in his hand again, this time more gently, and led her down the path toward the planes. "The pilot is expecting us."

Julia looked over her shoulder at the party. "What about your brothers?"

"They can find their own way home."

"And our things?"

"I had the pilot arrange for them to be brought to the plane."
Well, aren't you in a snit?

They were walking up the stairs of the private plane when Julia couldn't contain her displeasure any longer. "You're not going to tell me why we're leaving?"

He let go of her arm only when the outer hatch was closed. Julia took a seat near the window. Gio sat across from her. The plane took off with neither of them saying a word.

His eyes burned with passion and a darker emotion. "I should send you home on the next flight out of Rome. I should get as far away from you as I can—because when I'm with you I want the impossible."

"What happened at the party, Gio?"

"The truth was more disappointing than I was prepared for."

Julia undid her seat belt and crossed over to him. She sat sideways on his lap and looped her arms around his neck.

He tensed beneath her, and for a second Julia wondered if he was going to ask her to get off him, but he didn't. His arms closed around her, and he buried his face in her hair.

Julia pulled back and looked into his eyes. "You can tell me it's none of my business..."

"It's none of your business."

"And I don't need to know what you found out."

"I have no intention of telling you."

"But why not turn to your brothers? They were right there. You weren't alone at the party."

"There was no need to involve them."

"I have a feeling they're already involved, regardless of how much you keep from them."

"Are you done?" he asked and moved her hair aside so he could kiss the side of her neck.

She pushed at his chest. This was what he did. He used sex to distract her. *Does he really think he can distract me with—*

oh, that's nice. Gio pushed one strap of her dress aside and slid a hand inside the neckline, gently cupping her bare breast.

Focus. This is important. "You shouldn't shut people out just because things get complicated."

An excited shiver ran down her back as she felt the bulge of his erection begin to throb against her thighs. He unzipped the back of her dress and lowered it, exposing both her breasts to his eager mouth. She gave in to the pleasure of it and buried her hands deep in his hair, holding his head as his mouth teased and worshipped her. *We can continue this talk later.*

Across the cabin of the plane the attendant coughed nervously, and then Julia heard the sound of the cockpit door opening. What had she seen? It didn't matter. Nothing mattered as the heat of the moment enveloped both of them. Theirs was a need that overrode everything else, even modesty.

Gio picked Julia up and turned her so she straddled his lap, claiming her mouth possessively with his as he did. He pulled at both sides of her gown until the material was bunched around her waist. His deft fingers pushed the material of her silk panties aside and dove between her lower lips.

"I need you. Here. Now."

Julia hastily unbuttoned his shirt, pushing it aside so she could run her hands over his muscular chest and down his rock-hard abs. Between hot kisses, Julia said, "God, yes."

He claimed her mouth, plundering and demanding, all the while working her with his fingers until she was wet and eager for him. "Stand up," he ordered.

She did. She would have done anything for him in that moment.

"Take your dress off."

She pushed her dress the rest of the way down and stepped out of it, and her satin panties.

He laid a hand on her stomach. "You are so perfect."

He stood and also stripped, then pushed her down in the chair and pulled her forward so only the edge of her ass stopped her from falling to the floor at his feet. He sat in the chair across from her, and took his hard cock in his own hand. "I want to see you come for me, Julia."

Julia slid a hand into her own wet folds and rubbed her throbbing clit. She rubbed it with an increasing speed. Slowly at first, then faster and faster. As she did, she watched him stroke himself, up and down. Growing even larger.

She reached up and kneaded her own breast, imagining that it was his hand. Spread open before him, she felt his hot gaze on her sex like a caress. Her hand clenched as heat spread through her and she came to a shuddering orgasm while he watched.

He stood, sheathed himself in a condom then pulled her to her feet and turned her around so she was facing the chair. With one hand he bent her over. His first thrust was deep and powerful and she muffled her cries in her hand. He held her hips in place and thrust again. Deeper. Harder. Building heat and waves of pleasure on what she'd brought to herself.

Julia gripped the chair arms as he pounded into her from behind. He slowed and eased himself out, then thrust back into her, and she cried out again before she thought to muffle the sound. He repeated the move and she stopped caring who heard her. She wanted it again and again. When she finally came it was with such volume that she was sure someone would open the cockpit door to make sure they were still alive.

He joined her in the orgasm. Then withdrew, cleaned himself off, and pulled her into his lap.

She collapsed onto his bare chest, loving how his heart beat loudly in her ear... slowing as hers did when they both came regained their senses.

As sanity returned, so did Julia's questions. He gave his body to her freely, but when it came to his heart he still closed her out. She stood and put on her dress, adjusting it so it covered her once again. Gio disposed of the condom and refastened his own clothing. Both rumpled and flushed, they stood facing each other.

Julia asked, "Where are we going?"

He sat and pulled her back onto his lap, this time tucking her against his broad chest. "Venice."

The idea of visiting one of the few places of her dreams was enough to distract her. She sat up. "Are you serious? Oh, my God, Venice. I forgive you for making me miss the wedding." He didn't look nearly as happy as she did about the idea. "If you were hoping to take someone who wouldn't be excited about it, you picked the wrong woman. I've always dreamed of going there. The architecture. The bridges. The gondolas. I could orgasm again just thinking about it."

He gave her a small smile. "My competition is a city?"

Julia didn't deny it. "Only one. There is something about it that has always called to me."

He studied her face. "It called to my father, also. He owned a palazzo on the Grand Canal."

"A palace? Right on the main canal? Does your family still own it?"

"No."

She placed a hand lightly on one of his cheeks. "Help me understand, Gio. I'm trying to."

He looked out the plane window, collecting his thoughts before answering her. "I don't completely understand it myself. I swore I would never return to Venice, but when I'm with you the past matters to me again. The truth matters." He breathed in deeply, then said, "We should be landing soon. Tonight we'll stay in a hotel north of Venice. Tomorrow we'll take a water taxi into the city."

Julia closed her eyes to a rush of emotions she couldn't contain. She wanted to shake him and demand that he tell her what had upset him.

But she knew she'd lose him if she pushed him.

And she wasn't ready for that.

ଔ

The next morning, Julia stood beside Gio in the back of the water taxi as it sped across the lagoon toward Venice. The wind had whipped her long curls around until she'd rolled them into a ponytail and contained them with one hand. The taxi bounced in the waves, jostling her against Gio. He moved behind her, holding on to the wooden top of the boat with both hands and supporting her with his body. She smiled at him over her shoulder, and his breath caught in his throat.

She pointed to islands along the way with childlike enthusiasm. "What is that island?"

He studied the small, deserted island. "Isola Compalto?" He wasn't sure.

She gave him a funny look. "You don't know?"

He shrugged and shook his head. "I'm not a fan of Venice or Venetians. I don't see the point. Why pour so much energy into something that was doomed from the start? So what if it sinks into the ocean? Build another city on better stilts, if that's what you want, but don't whine about the water if you choose to live in the middle it."

Julia turned so she was facing him. "You are completely missing the point of Venice."

A wave tossed her forward and rubbed her against him. "Which is?" he asked huskily, not actually caring about the answer, but loving how her face lit up at his question. If pretending to care kept her in his arms and smiling, he would listen to her read a dissertation on the history of every bridge in the city.

"It's a city that shouldn't have been. It should have failed a hundred times over. The wooden pillars they built it on should have rotted away, but the clay beneath the city protects it. Everything about Venice is a battle with nature. The soil is full of salt, so if you wanted to plant something, you had to bring in your own dirt, your own seeds, and protect both from the very place you planted it on. A place that is struggling so desperately just to survive shouldn't care about beauty, but it does."

"How do you know all this?"

"I love to read travel blogs," she said. "They say that if you want to make Venetians smile, give them a flower. Because a flower doesn't serve any purpose outside of bringing a person joy. And some would ask if a flower is then worth the effort. A Venetian would tell you that it is. That those simple pleasures are worth any price."

Julia's words cut through Gio. He was confused with his own choice to run to the same city where his father had found refuge. Could he find his own answers there?

What do I do with this burning anger? How do I stop it from consuming me?

Julia wants me to believe in love, but how can I when everywhere I look I see a twisted version of it?

An impatient frown creased Julia's brow. "If you don't intend to enjoy yourself at all, why are we here? Why come to this amazing place and choose to be miserable? Because it is a choice, Gio."

She looked up at him from beneath her long lashes and, right then, he chose her. "I'll play tourist with you for a day, Julia, on one condition."

"That is?"

"We leave everything else behind us. Just you and me in Venice. Come away with me, Julia. Let's leave all this behind." His phone rang in his breast pocket. He took it out and groaned. "That's Luke. Probably wants to know where we are."

Julia grabbed his phone and threw it into the lagoon. When he opened his mouth to say something she put her hand over his mouth softly. "Step one to running away—no phones." Then she smiled. "Before you get upset, now we're even."

The irritation he expected to feel didn't surface. Instead, it was as if she'd cut him free from suffocating tethers. No one knew he was in Venice. No one expected him back at his office. He wanted to lose himself in Julia—not just in her body, but in the full experience of her. He pulled her roughly against him and kissed her until they were both shaking with need.

The driver turned and called back to them. "Do you still want me to stop, or would you like me to circle around?"

Gio raised his head and looked into Julia's eyes. "What do you want to see?"

She smiled up at him. "Everything."

He addressed the driver. "Do you give guided tours? It's her first time here."

The driver shrugged one shoulder. "Me? No. I don't do the tour so much."

Gio said, "I'll pay you triple whatever you charge."

A large smile spread across the driver's face. "Ah, then coming up is the Rialto Bridge. There is a bar nearby, very nice. You look at the ceiling and all you see are women's... how do you say... bras? Tell them I sent you. On your left is a hotel that if you go by at night sometimes the women, they don't close the shutters. I don't judge, I just enjoy."

A chuckle rumbled deep within Gio. He met Julia's eyes and said, "He did say he doesn't normally give tours."

Julia smiled up at him. "I can't imagine why not."

They laughed together as the taxi driver continued to give them insider tips that were surely not mentioned in more formal tours.

After the boat tour, Gio walked with Julia up and down a maze of streets. They crossed bridges. They stopped for gelato. They laughed as they watched young American children chasing pigeons in St. Mark's Square.

Julia enthusiastically asked a fellow tourist for directions to the Gallerie dell'Accademia and headed off with Gio to find it. They wandered in and out of the many shops along the way. Julia stopped frequently to study a feature of a building or to share a factoid she'd read about Venetians battling the rising waters and its effect on their homes. It was a day out of time, and even though Gio knew it couldn't last, he felt happier than he had since his father had passed.

When they eventually found the museum, they spent a couple of hours viewing its extensive collection of Venetian and European paintings. It was early afternoon when they reentered the sunshine and the crowded streets. Just outside the museum,

they found a wooden bridge that arched across the Grand Canal.
Julia paused at the top of it, and Gio stopped beside her. "Have
you ever seen anything more beautiful?" she asked without
looking away from the view.

Gio didn't answer. He'd spent too many years hating the city
to ever truly find it beautiful. The day had given him one
answer, though. It was possible to find pleasure in denial.

So, perhaps he was more like his father than he knew.

Which was not good news.

☙

Julia glanced over her shoulder expecting to see Gio smiling,
but instead she caught him fighting back whatever inner demon
he denied having. "What are you thinking about, Gio?"

"Nothing," he said dismissively.

Julia chewed her bottom lip. "I thought you were enjoying
this as much as I am."

He stood behind her, pushed the hair off the back of her
neck, and kissed her gently. "I was enjoying you."

"So, you've been humoring me all day?"

He turned her in his arms. "Let's not argue. It doesn't
matter."

His words were a cold slap of reality. "It matters to me. I
want to know how you really feel."

"Do you?" He looked down at the structure they stood on
and shook his head in disgust. "Take a good look at what we're
standing on. Wood over hideous steel. A façade to keep the
tourists happy. You want the truth? It's ugly. Fake."

Julia froze in his arms. "Like our day here?" she asked
softly.

He didn't deny it.

"Like us?" Julia searched his face for some hint of how he
felt. "You asked me to leave it all behind and I tried to. I tried to
tell myself it's okay that you don't want to tell me what
happened on the island—that you don't want to tell me

anything. These last few weeks have been amazing, but you shut me out of everything that's important. What are we doing together, Gio? Are we working towards something, or am I just this summer's entertainment?"

Still he held his silence.

"Say something." She pushed him away with both hands, then stood in front of him, chest heaving with emotion. "I keep waiting for you to open up to me. I keep thinking that if I give you more time you'll let me in. But you're not going to, are you?"

"What do you want me to say, Julia?" The coldness of his tone tore into her.

Her eyes filled with tears. "Just the truth. Do you love me?"

He opened his mouth, then closed it with a snap.

Well, there is my answer. "I can't do this. I can't stay with you knowing that I'm the only one who is going to mourn this when it ends. I'm sorry, Gio. This is my fault. You're exactly the man you said you were. We need to end this before you break my heart." She took a step backward, away from him.

"It was a mistake to bring you to the wedding... and to Venice. We'll fly back to the States tonight. Once we're back in New York this will all blow over."

"I am flying home, but not with you. It wasn't the wedding or Venice. It's you. You don't get it, and I can't explain it better than I have. Good-bye, Gio."

"You're going to leave over this?"

"Yes," she said. "Because in the end you can't give me the one thing I want from you." She stepped away from him. "I'll take a taxi boat back to the airport. Please send my things back to me in New York."

"No," he said firmly.

"Don't, Gio. Don't make this difficult. I need to go home."

"We'll fly back together."

She shook her head. She wanted to hate him, but she couldn't. He wanted to love her. She could see it in his eyes. He wasn't ready to love anyone. That was what he'd tried to tell her, but she hadn't wanted to hear it. "No. There was a reason you came to Italy. I don't know what you're looking for, Gio, but find it. Find those answers. Maybe then you'll understand what I'm asking you for. And if that happens, come find me."

"Julia—"

Julia turned and walked quickly away. She didn't want to give him a chance to change her mind. She didn't want something that looked good on the surface.

She wanted it all.

Chapter Twenty-One

WITH JULIA'S WORDS echoing in his head, Gio stood in the small courtyard behind his father's old palazzo. It looked as if every part of it was in need of repair. He wondered if it had looked the same nine years earlier when a younger him had stood in that same spot the day he'd come to collect his father's remains.

He didn't remember many details from that day, just the anger and hurt that had filled him. He wouldn't have described his parents' marriage as warm, but he'd been unprepared for the reality of how little his father had respected it.

While waiting for the paperwork to be completed, his father's mistress had asked to speak to him. He remembered being enraged by the audacity of her request. He didn't want to speak to her. He didn't want her to exist at all.

His mother had predicted that Leora would try to pull him aside. She'd warned Gio that such a woman would say anything to milk them for more money than she'd already taken from his father. "Don't think she's above blackmail, George," his mother had said. "She may threaten to tell her story. You have to keep this out of the papers. The company will suffer enough from your father's passing. A scandal could do real damage." Whether her tears were born from anger or loss, Gio didn't know, but that had been the only time he'd ever seen his mother cry. "I couldn't handle the shame on top of losing your father. Make it go away, George. Please. Make sure no one ever knows about her."

And so he'd refused to listen to anything Leora had tried to tell him that day. Instead, he'd threatened to bring the full force of his connections down upon her if she ever spoke of her relationship with his father. She was worried about losing the house, even though his father had promised to leave it to her. He'd assured her that no one was interested in it unless they heard her name again. If they did, he would utilize every lawyer on their payroll to break the will. She would be left with nothing. Unless she kept her silence.

He'd always believed he'd done the right thing. Until now.

He hadn't told his brothers because he'd wanted to protect them from the truth. He'd heard part of a row once between Nick and their mother that sounded as if Nick knew something. Or suspected. Nick had been confronting their mother about her role in it, which Gio had never understood. No woman deserved the humiliation of discovering her husband had another woman on the side.

Whatever their mother's response had been, Nick had been furious afterward. Gio had sworn to his mother that he would never tell anyone about Leora, so even when pressed for answers by Nick, he'd kept the truth to himself.

If I did the right thing, why does it all feel so wrong?

What's real and what's a lie?

I don't know anymore.

The door at the top of the stairs opened and Gio was faced, for the second time, with his father's mistress. This time, however, he saw her as a person and not the embodiment of his father's betrayal. She was modestly dressed in a blue cotton blouse and matching skirt. Her short hair curled and framed a face that, had he not spent so many years despising, he would have said had aged well. She had a classic, simple beauty, without the artificial enhancements he was used to seeing in women her age.

Was it that beauty that had drawn his father to her? Brought him back to her year after year? What was here that had been worth risking everything—marriage, children, fortune?

He was so lost in the past he didn't realize she was speaking to him. "Gio? Is that you?"

He froze.

She beckoned him to come closer. "It is you. Come. Come inside."

At any other time in his life, Gio would have said something cutting and left. But Julia was right. He'd come to Italy for answers, and he wouldn't find them if he walked away. "I wouldn't have thought you'd be very pleased to see me."

She opened the door wider. "I've waited a long time for you to return."

He walked up the palazzo's stone stairs and followed her through the back door of the house and into a salon. The experience was like stepping back into time. From the heavy tapestries on the floor to the ornate wooden ceilings, it was obvious that efforts had been made to retain the charm of the seventeenth-century palace. The furniture was all made from dark wood—simple pieces with worn cloth cushions. But the house was immaculately clean, with no evidence of house staff.

Gio noticed pictures of him and his brothers scattered around the home. On the walls, on the mantel. Everywhere people normally put photos of their family. Nearly ten years after his father's death. Gio couldn't understand it. He walked around the room and studied the photos. His father was in many of them, laughing with his boys.

In one photo, the one that stopped Gio in his tracks, his father was holding a baby. Gio looked over his shoulder at Leora.

She nodded and said softly, "That's my daughter, Gigi."

"How old is she now?" Gio asked.

"Twenty and away at college. I borrowed monies against this house, but she's worth it."

Gio found another photo of his father and the girl, when she was about ten, holding his father's hand and smiling up at him. "Was she? Is she?" He wasn't sure how to ask.

He wasn't sure he wanted to know.

"Yes, she's your half sister. She has your father's eyes. As do you."

"Does she know?"

"That you're related? Yes. She's always known."

Gio took one of the photos of her off the wall and held it out in question. "And you never told anyone?" So many emotions were rushing through him he wasn't sure how he felt.

Leora asked, "Are you hungry? Thirsty?"

"No," Gio said and a sick feeling came over him. "She wasn't a secret, was she?"

Leora smoothed her hands down her plain dress. "Your mother had every right to hate me and any child we made. I understood that. Your father loved Patrice, so I did also. I kept my silence out of respect for her."

Gio laid the photo down on the mantel. "Living with another woman's husband doesn't fit any definition of love or respect I'm aware of."

Leora picked up the photo he'd put down and placed it back where it belonged. "Your mother has always been a complicated woman. She didn't love your father. She tried to, but she couldn't fool herself or him."

Gio turned his back to Leora and looked out the window, seeing but not seeing the boats passing on the Grand Canal below. "Isn't that what all married men tell the women they screw on the side? That their wives don't love them?"

"Maybe," she said softly. "But in this case, it was true. I have nothing to prove to you, Gio. No reason to lie to you. Your mother is a very unhappy woman. She has been for a long time. Happiness is a choice, you know. Like love. You either open yourself up to it or you don't. Your mother could never let the past go long enough to see what all that anger was costing her. She let a man who loved her slip away to Venice. A man who would have gone back to her if she'd ever let him into her heart." The words were too similar to those Julia had used for him not to be shaken by them.

He turned back to face her, unable to conceal the bitterness in his voice. "My father made a second family here because he loved my mother so much? Pardon me if I find your take on the scenario tainted by your desire to make it palatable."

Leora looked at him sadly. "Believe what you want, but Gio loved your mother, and he loved you and your brothers."

"Why do you call him Gio? He went by George."

With memories luring her away for a moment, Leora said, "Not when he was here in Italy. In the States, he was who he thought your mother needed him to be. He may have even been happy in that American lifestyle for a while. But in his heart he was always Gio." She smiled at him warmly. "Here he laughed louder, worried less about what others thought of him, and enjoyed the simple pleasures—like being a father."

"Father to a bastard child."

Leora shrugged. "Call Gigi what you want, but it won't change what we had. Your father loved us. Just as he loved you."

When Gio said nothing, Leora walked over to a shelf and took down a leather-bound book. "Do you think your father loved you less because he had us?" She handed him the large book. "He kept a scrapbook of you and your brothers. He would sit with Gigi and tell her stories about all of you. He promised one day he would introduce her to you and she would have a large family, as he'd always had."

Gio reluctantly took the book and opened it angrily. His father had filled page after page with the story of his sons' childhoods. There were clippings from articles they had been mentioned in, along with notes describing why the event had been important. He closed the book abruptly. "Why didn't he?"

"Only your father could truly answer that question. Or perhaps your mother." She studied his face and asked, "Tell me, Gio, why do you choose to use the Italian version of your name? Who are you in your heart?"

"I'm not my father," Gio said defensively. He thought back to the summer he'd chosen to no longer go by George. It had been during one of his visits to Isola Santos. His cousins had called him by the name and it had felt right. So right that nearly no one called him George anymore. *God, how could I have forgotten? All this time I told myself that I hated them, even as I hung on to the one thing they gave me.*

My name.

"We are all our parents in one way or another, Gio. The best and the worst of them. Find the good in your father, Gio, and forgive him for what he's not here to explain to you. And don't judge your mother too harshly. We don't know what closed her heart."

Gio was coming to the uncomfortable realization that after ten years of fearing that he would end up like his father—he'd become something worse.

He was as bitter and closed off as his mother.

And it had cost him just as it had cost her.

It may very well have robbed him of the only woman he could imagine spending the rest of his life with. *Julia.*

He looked Leora in the eye and asked, "Would you mind if I contact Gigi?"

"I would love that."

Gio walked around the room again, studying the photos of his family and hers. "My brothers don't know about you. I thought it was better for them if they didn't. I was wrong. I'll tell them about you now. About both of you."

"You are always welcome here, Gio. Your brothers, too."

Hitting an overload of emotions, Gio made his excuses and left—promising to return. He walked back to the bridge where Julia had left him and stood there for a long time, replaying the day in his head.

❧

An hour later, Gio stepped out of a hired car onto a private airfield. The pilot met him and asked where he wanted to go, but Gio didn't answer.

"Wherever Julia went," didn't feel like a sane answer. Was she still in Italy, or on her way back to New York?

A limo pulled up beside them and all four of the doors opened simultaneously.

"Looks like we got here just in time," Luke said.

Gio shook his head in surprise. "What are all of you doing here?"

A tall blond man stepped out of the car and said, "We came to find you."

Gio's eyebrows rose at the sight of the would-be groom. "Don't you have somewhere to be?"

Stephan smiled sadly. "We postponed the wedding until tomorrow. Nicole understands why we had to."

Gio looked from cousin to brothers and back. "I don't."

Stephan took an envelope out of his pocket and bounced it in his hand as if he were weighing it before offering it. "I found myself in a tricky spot this past summer. A close brush with my own mortality changed the way I look at many things."

Gio took the envelope. He opened it and read the contents. His name was clearly printed on the top of the deed for Isola Santos.

"I can't take this," he said, his voice thick with emotion.

"I don't want it. It should have gone to you. Just be careful, Gio. I spent years chasing it. I thought it was important. It's just a rock in the ocean. It doesn't matter. Nicole is what's important to me now. And my family."

A rush of emotion filled Gio. Stephan wasn't pretending to care about him.

He did.

There was so much he wanted to say to him. So much he needed to tell his brothers. He didn't know where to start. "Perhaps we could be the first generation to share the island. You can have Dominic's side."

Stephan choked on a laugh. "That's cruel."

In a more serious tone, Gio said, "I was wrong to leave your wedding. Wrong about more than I can even begin to explain now."

Stephan put a hand on Gio's shoulder and said, "You are not the first Andrade to make a mistake, and you won't be the last."

"Speaking of mistakes..." Max looked around and asked, "Did you lose Julia?"

Gio shrugged one shoulder unhappily. "She went back to New York."

Luke shook his head. "That's a shame."

An uncharacteristically sympathetic Nick said, "We liked her."

"She said I wasn't ready."

"And what did you say when she said that?" Nick asked.

Gio shrugged again. "What could I say?"

Nick turned to his cousin. "We can't lose Julia. I actually like Gio when he's around her."

Luke broke the silence that followed his brother's declaration by asking, "How far could she have gotten?"

Max looked at Gio. "Is she on a commercial flight?"

"Just call her. Maybe she's not on the plane yet," Max suggested.

"I broke her phone. And even if she had it, her number is in mine, which is on the bottom of the ocean," Gio said in frustration.

Luke looked at his oldest brother with a funny expression on his face. "I'm ready to diagnose you, Gio."

"What the hell are you talking about?"

"You have a severe case of, 'In love with no fucking idea of what to do about it.' " He shook his head sadly. "It's the worst I've seen."

"She wanted to leave," Gio defended himself, even as he kicked himself for letting her leave. "What was I supposed to do? Kidnap her?"

Stephan shrugged. "I've seen it work."

Max said, "And Gio thinks I hang out with a questionable crowd?"

Stephan asked, "Do you love her?"

There were many things that Gio was no longer certain about, but he knew the answer to that question. "Yes, I do."

"Then go get her. Tell her you love her. Everything else will work out."

A ray of hope lit and grew within Gio. Could it be that easy? Could he choose love? "You're right. I have to tell her how I feel. I'm going back to New York. I wish I knew what flight she was on." He looked at his cousin in apology. "It'll mean I'll miss your wedding, but I have to find her."

Stephan groaned. "I know someone who can find out anything. He could probably tell us if she's en route or at the airport. He can access almost any database."

"You mean a hacker?"

"He doesn't like that term, but yes." Stephan made a brief phone call, then said, "She has a two-hour layover in Rome."

Determination filled Gio. "I still have time."

"Just make sure you're back for the ceremony tomorrow," Stephan said in resignation. "Or Nicole will kill me."

Gio hesitated before he left. He looked at his three smiling brothers and said, "I know I haven't always been that easy to get along with, but when I get back we need to talk. I need to make some things right."

Nick made a face at Luke. "Why does love make you sound so much like you're dying?"

ଔ

Julia used some of her time in the airport to check her phone messages via a public phone—an expensive necessity. She needed to reconnect with her life. *Now.* Her father had called twice. He said there was nothing important but asked that she call when she had time.

She had a couple of messages from friends back in Rhode Island who were wondering how New York was treating her. Only her closest friends were going to hear the real story, and even then she wasn't sure she'd be able to talk about any of the past week for a long time.

What are the five stages of realizing you just did something too stupid to tell your friends?

Denial: It was not a bad idea to run away to a foreign country with a man I barely know.

Anger: Until he turned out to be a complete jackass who didn't fall in love instantly the way everyone does in books.

Bargaining: I'll never do anything like this again if I can just fall out of love with him as fast as I fell in love.

Depression: I can't believe I did this. I told myself not to. I knew it would end badly, but that didn't stop me, did it? Instead of doing something important—like saving my family's company—I go off and get my heart broken by someone who told me he wasn't looking for anything serious.

But do I listen?

No, I see only what I want to see.

Acceptance? Not likely to happen for a while.

Julia hit the button for the final message. She'd half hoped it would be from Gio, but it was a woman whose voice she didn't recognize. "Hello, my name is Lisa. I'm Mrs. Rockport's personal assistant. I'm calling on her behalf to invite you to her house next week. She's received so many compliments on your necklace that she'd like to commission it in gold and diamonds as well as look at your other designs."

Julia played the message a second time, and then a third.

I did it.

I found my buyer.

She called her father to tell him. He was happy, but not surprised. He said he always knew she would sell them. She promised to start sending him money as soon as it came in and, just as she knew he would, her father told her it wasn't necessary.

"Dad, I'll be able to come back now. I can help you figure out the books and work everything out with the bank."

"You don't have to, Julia. I accepted a buyout offer."

"Oh, Dad. No."

"It's okay, Julia. It's what I wanted. I was hanging on to my factory because I didn't want to let my employees go. But the new owner says he'll keep everyone on. I have some money in the bank now and more time to be with your mother. This was for the best."

The news was bittersweet to Julia. "I'll come see you next weekend, Dad."

"We'll be here, honey."

Julia hung up the phone and fought back the wave of sadness that filled her. She couldn't imagine her family without their furniture store.

It also meant there was no longer any reason for her to be in New York. She could create Mrs. Rockport's orders anywhere. She could return to her apartment in the city, but she wouldn't be happy there. Not without Gio.

Her flight number was called and Julia walked to her gate. The attendant looked at her ticket, then let her through. Although Julia was lost in thought, she stopped midway down the enclosed ramp and noted that no one was behind her. She hadn't seen anyone in line in front of her either.

Maybe I'm early?

No, they said it was time to board.

The stewardess at the plane ushered her forward, which put her somewhat at ease. Julia stopped again before the plane door and looked over her shoulder again.

Did I actually think he would come after me?

I'm hopeless.

With that, Julia stepped through the door of the plane. It was empty. She looked around and gasped. Every seat in first class was overflowing with pink roses. She walked down the aisle. Every seat in the next section was also covered with pink roses. She stood in the middle of the plane and started to cry.

"When I pictured this moment, I didn't imagine you crying," Gio said from behind her.

Julia spun. She wanted to run and throw herself in his arms, but she was afraid. Afraid to have her heart broken for a second time that day.

He walked to her and held out a hand, but she stood frozen in place. He let his hand drop to his side and said, "I've been an ass."

Julia nodded, wiping the tears from her cheeks.

"I'm not good at talking about how I feel."

Still Julia silently watched and waited.

"I thought I was happy before I met you, Julia. But I wasn't. I was comfortable with being miserable. That's not the same thing. I didn't want to change. I didn't think I could." He stepped closer to her and took one of her hands in his. "You told me that I wouldn't let you in, and you were right. I had gotten used to closing myself off. I forgot how to let anyone in."

Julia gave his hand a supportive squeeze and held his eyes.

"I didn't find all the answers I was looking for in Venice, Julia, but I learned something about myself."

"You did?" Fresh tears poured down Julia's cheeks.

"Yes. I don't want to repeat the mistakes my parents made. I don't want to spend my life hiding what I feel."

Julia laid a hand on Gio's cheek and smiled up at him through her tears. "And how is that?"

"I love you, Julia. I can't promise that life with me with be easy, or that you won't need to walk me through some of this, but I can promise you that no one will ever love you more than I do." He kissed her with all the love he'd been holding back, and the last of Julia's fears fell away.

When their kiss broke off, she said, "I love you, too, Gio."

"I should have told you what happened on the island. I was angry and I'm used to burying those feelings."

"What happened?"

He hugged her to him, tucked her beneath his chin, and said, "Alessandro told me that my mother had returned the deed for the island to him. She'd told him we didn't want the island. All this time I hated him for thinking I wasn't one of them enough to give it to me, when it was my mother who didn't want me to have it."

Julia hugged him tightly. "Why would she do that?"

Gio shook his head sadly. "I don't know. She never liked my father's family. That's actually putting it mildly. She couldn't tolerate being around them at all. Apparently her hatred of them took priority over the feelings of her sons."

"I'm so sorry to hear that."

"I'm not." He kissed her forehead. "I needed to know the truth. I was trapped in all the lies. Suffocating beneath them. My brother was right—I needed that smack with a lamp. I needed to wake up."

"What will you do now?"

"I'm not entirely sure, but I know that we can figure it out together."

"We... I like that. It still doesn't feel real. Are you really here?"

"I sure hope so, or I paid all of the passengers from this plane a lot of money to find alternate flights for nothing."

She pulled back in surprise and asked, "You paid everyone to take another flight?"

He pulled her against him again. "You're marrying a very rich man. I get what I want."

Julia's stomach did a somersault at his words. Did he just say? Did he just ask? "Was that a proposal?"

He raised one eyebrow—at first neither confirming nor denying. "You know I don't ask when the outcome isn't in question."

"And what makes you think—"

He cut off her question with a kiss that left them both breathless. "I don't think. I know. You're marrying me, Julia. I can't imagine my life without you in it."

She raised her hand and touched his cheek softly. "Well, I suppose if I have no choice."

"Absolutely none."

"What am I going to do with you?"

A lusty smile spread across his face. "I have plenty of ideas."

She shook her head and laughed. "Here on this plane?"

He took her by the hand again. "My plane is refueling now."

"Where to this time?"

"Anywhere you want to go."

"It's a shame we missed the wedding."

"We didn't miss anything. They postponed it until tomorrow."

"For you?"

"For us."

"We should go back."

He nuzzled her neck. "Tomorrow. Tonight, come away with me, Julia, one more time. We'll find a quiet place. Just you and me."

She hopped with excitement beside him, then stopped as a thought suddenly came to her. "Hey, I finally sold some of my jewelry pieces. Can you believe it?"

He pulled her close and hugged her. "With you, Julia, I believe in everything again."

Epilogue

MADDY D'ARGENSON WATCHED Nicole Corisi spin in her Marchesa wedding gown before a floor-length mirror in her bedroom suite. The amazing white gown was long-sleeved with a high neckline and lace bodice, the skirt layered in silk organza with tulle petals. Her long black hair was confined to a tight chignon on the crown of her head that would soon sport a long veil.

Nicole was radiant, smiling, and beautiful in a way only a bride can be.

Maddy sat on the edge of a chaise lounge, happy Nicole had allowed each attendant to choose her own style of bridesmaid gown. She'd chosen a figure-forgiving empire-waist chiffon one. She wasn't sure she would have fit into something with less give, considering how her stomach had seemed to double in size in a way it hadn't for her first pregnancy. "My father and Uncle Victor are already arguing over names for your first child. Are you sure you want to do this?"

Looking over her shoulder at Maddy, Nicole smiled. "I love your family."

"Our family," Maddy said seriously. "It's about time that you're officially part of it, too. Stephan should have married you the first time around. Uncle Victor should have never gotten involved."

"He meant well," Nicole defended her future father-in-law.

"He was wrong to try to break you up. At least he finally apologized." Maddy placed a hand on her stomach as her baby kicked. "If you ask him, he still says he did it because he cares about you and thought his son needed time to grow up. I hope I don't ever meddle in my children's lives like that."

"You? Meddle? Never," Nicole said, tongue in cheek. In a more serious tone, she continued, "It was easy to forgive Victor. He did it out of love. You have no idea how lucky you are that you have a family who cares so much about each other."

Maddy made a sympathetic face. "You have your brother, Dominic, and his wife. They both love you. You've mended your relationship with your mother. You have family who loves you—today all you're doing is doubling the number of them."

Nicole cocked her head to one side.

"Okay, quadrupling them," Maddy amended. "You know what I mean."

"I do." Turning to face the mirror again, Nicole tucked a loose lock back into place. "You'll never know how grateful I am to your family. You not only gave me Stephan, but you also brought my brother back into my life. I want to cry every time I think about him walking me down the aisle. This whole day is better than I ever dared dream it could be. I might throw up." With a shy smile, Nicole said, "Is every bride this nervous? Are they all afraid to wake up and discover it was a dream?"

"You cannot vomit on a dress that beautiful." Maddy chuckled. "And don't worry. This is real. If it were your dream it wouldn't have been postponed a day."

Nicole turned, clasping her hands nervously in front of her. "I understood why Stephan asked me to. He couldn't let his cousins leave upset." Nicole looked out the window. "He brought them all back. Even Gio. I heard he flew in this morning."

"He would have returned last night, but he and Julia had quarreled. Looks like they made up because she came back with him."

Nicole smoothed the skirt of her gown. "I really like her."

"And?"

"And he looks happy when he's with her."

"And?"

Nicole shook her head in confusion.

Maddy gave her an impish grin and a triumphant wiggle. "You can say it—I was right about her."

Nicole laughed delicately and nodded in concession. "You were definitely right. She's probably still a little afraid of you since you practically kidnapped her to introduce her to me, but your idea that helping Gio and his brothers find love might bring them back to the family seems to be working. At least with Gio."

A light knock on the door announced the arrival of the other women in Nicole's bridal party, each dressed in similarly colored dresses of different lengths and styles.

Abby Corisi rushed over and hugged her sister-in-law. "You look stunning."

Abby's sister, Lil Walton, followed suit and gave Nicole a bone-crushing embrace. "I didn't think I could be happier than I was at my wedding, but I will probably bawl through this whole ceremony. Every time I think about you almost losing Stephan this summer, I get goose bumps. I mean, to have gone through so much and then..."

"Lil," several of the women in the room said in unison to halt her from saying more, then realized what they had done and burst into laughter.

Lil stepped back and smiled sheepishly. "What I mean to say is—enjoy every moment of today. You two have earned it."

Nicole chuckled. She'd grown to love Lil's impulsive bouts of honesty. She looked around the room and grateful tears came to her eyes. After a lonely childhood, to be part of this large and loving family was more than she'd ever dared wish for. She hugged Lil tightly. "I knew what you meant, and thank you."

Lil plopped onto the chaise lounge beside Maddy. "So, about our bet. I see only one of the Andrade cousins brought a date. Was she anyone's? Alethea and I planted an IT ex-swimsuit model we thought would be perfect for Gio, but apparently he'd already met—what's her name again? Julia?"

"Yes, Julia," said Abby. "I spoke to her this morning and she and Gio are engaged. No ring yet, and they don't plan to announce anything until after the wedding, but isn't that exciting?" Then she looked at her sister and asked, "What do you mean, 'planted an IT person'?"

Lil looked away at the ceiling as she said, "We didn't do anything illegal. We just made a few phone calls. Cogent had an opening. If everyone else's online résumés disappeared, is that so bad?" Lil's expression turned skeptical. "Are you honestly telling me that you didn't plant anyone?"

Nicole jumped in with a smile. "Engaged. I knew it would happen fast for them the moment I saw them together. But don't try to look all innocent, Abby. You had to have planted someone. Even Maddy and I did. Although we didn't think Gio would be the first one to cave. We found an amazing woman who is going to school to work with young children and has a chauffer's license. We thought she'd be perfect for Nick, but she was transferred to another department of Cogent soon after being hired."

"Marie and I thought Nick would be the easiest one, too," Abby finally admitted. "We gave his normal secretary a position at Corisi Enterprises and sent over someone we loved. She was efficient and adorable but she was transferred also. I've spoken to her, though, since then and she says she loves her new job. I think we all will have to be more subtle with our next one."

Lil snapped her fingers. "So Julia was an independent choice. Looks like none of us won this one."

Maddy stood and crossed to the window. She looked down at Gio and Julia standing with her father. Nick, Luke, and Max were mingling with the other guests. Her heart swelled with hope. "I'd count this as a win for all of us."

Nicole joined her by the window and nodded. "I know exactly what you mean."

Meeting Nicole's eyes, Maddy said, "I just wish I'd been able to convince their mother to come. She seemed interested when I told her about Julia. I thought she'd like to know her son had finally met someone."

Abby joined them. "You didn't tell me that you went to see Gio's mother. How did that go? I thought you said she and your family didn't get along well."

Maddy shrugged sadly. "They don't. I wish I knew why. I told her that Stephan and I were actively trying to mend our relationship with her sons. I'd hoped she would join them here this weekend."

Nicole said, "I don't know, Maddy. I'm not sure she wants the family back together."

Maddy raised her chin stubbornly. "I disagree. She invited me to come see her again. I don't know what happened between her and my uncles, but she definitely wanted to hear more about our bet."

With a gasp, Nicole raised a hand to her mouth. "You told her?"

"I thought she might want to help," Maddy said defensively. "Luke says that his mother has always felt like an outsider in our family. She needs to know that we trust her."

Nicole looked down at the wedding party again and said softly, "I hope you know what you're doing, Maddy."

Confidently, Maddy said, "I do." She turned away from the window and said, "How are we on time?"

Abby said, "We should start heading down now if we want any pictures before the ceremony."

As they gathered up their accessories, Nicole walked over to her soon-to-be sister and said, "Maddy, this is your family. I don't mean to question how you deal with them."

Maddy hugged Nicole and said, "No, it's our family. You've been an Andrade for a while now—today simply makes it legal. I understand why you don't trust people, Nicole, but I'm right about this. Trust me. Patrice Stanfield needs to know we care about her. Then she'll come around."

Nicole glanced back over her shoulder at the window and said, "I hope you're right, Maddy. I really hope you're right.

The End

Can't wait to read the next book in The Andrades Series?

Go to RuthCardello.com and add your email to the mailing list.

We'll send you an email as soon as the next book is released!

Made in the USA
Lexington, KY
03 January 2016